SILVER CHAINS

SARAH URQUHART

SILVER CHAINS is a work of fiction. Names, characters, and places are products of the author's imagination or used fictitiously. Any resemblance to locales or persons, living or dead, is coincidental.

Cover design by Untold Designs

This book is a steamy, small town, shifter romance and is for mature audiences only. It contains sexually explicit scenes and adult language that may be offensive to some readers.

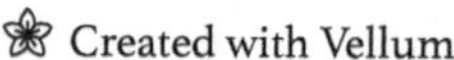 Created with Vellum

To my beta readers.

ACKNOWLEDGMENTS

This story didn't come easy, and I have to thank my family most of all for being supportive, allowing me the time and space I needed to write Zachary's story. Friends that came to the rescue and helped by being working partners and/or childcare. It takes a village and I have one. And I have to thank my beta readers most of all. Carrie and Jadzia, you both came through for me. Your comments and suggestions are always appreciated. This book wouldn't have been released on time if it weren't for your help. Thank you.

Austin made the hole bigger in his sandbox. He'd been digging for at least an hour, needing to make the pit where his truck would crash as big as he could.

"Ten more minutes, Austin. It's almost time for bed." His mom called from the deck, wiping her hands on a dish towel. Austin doubled his efforts, determined to finish his pit, the home for all the broken trucks.

The breeze picked up, but he ignored it. He was on a mission. Tomorrow, he'd race his monster trucks on the sand track he'd made and any that lost the race would have to jump over the pit, some sure to fall below spending the rest of their days in the hole. He laughed to himself over his evil plan.

If only he could finish the pit before he had to go to bed.

His hair blew into his eyes. He shook his head, but the wind blew it back down. Austin huffed and kept digging.

It was the end of summer, but the days were still long and bright, and his bedtime later than normal. So when it darkened above him, his sand pit in shadow, Austin looked up. And up, tilting his head all the way back to see a puff of grey smoke above his head. His mouth held open in an 'o' as he stared at the motionless cloud.

Austin moved to the side to look around the grey puff. Blue with small white clouds filled the sky, the sun lower and despite that, the evening was bright. He stood and took three steps back, putting himself outside of his sandbox and out from under the cloud. One. Two. Three. The cloud dispersed, turning into twirls of smoke, creating patterns in the air. The patterns turned into shapes, then formed animals. Wolves, bears, and large birds played together in the air.

He didn't know what it was or why it was here, but it looked cool. The smoke moved away from him, up the hill, away from his house, still creating patterns and playful animals. Austin followed. It picked up speed and so did Austin. He didn't want to lose it. He was panting by the time he reached the top of the hill, and the smoke turned right to weave through the trees. Austin slowed his progress to balance on rocks and step over branches and roots.

The further he went, the fewer trees surrounded him and the ground became easier to hike over. The smoke stopped in an open space and waited for Austin to catch up. When he stopped, it rushed over him, twirling at his feet then up and around him. Austin realized it wasn't smoke at all. It was wind, warm wind.

He chased it around in a circle, his laughter echoing. He jumped to catch it, only to have the warmth circle his hand and move away, as if to say *down low, too slow*.

Austin giggled and kept running, determined to catch it again. Just as he reached for it a second time, he tripped, falling to the ground, catching himself with his forearms. He winced, holding back the tears. The heel of his hand and his elbow stung. His eyes welled and he blinked. There was no point in crying when his mom wasn't here to help.

He looked back to see what he'd tripped over and gasped. Grey fur crouched on the ground. A small head turned with grey eyes, the colour of the wind, stared at him. The baby wolf, a pup, stood and wagged his tail. When Austin didn't get up, the pup tilted his head.

Austin swiveled, trying to find other pups or the mother, but there was nothing. He stood and eyed the pup. The wind had disappeared. What should he do now?

The pup seemed to have an idea. He crouched down, ready to play. He yipped and bounced until Austin gave in. With no other wolves near, he joined the pup and bounced around with him. They chased each other, playing a form of tag.

The wind came back and joined their game, chasing them, then running from them. Austin forgot he was supposed to be home getting ready for bed.

The grey swirls chased and reached out, catching Austin and the wolf pup at the same time. It wrapped them together in a warm grasp. Austin laughed. But after a moment, something didn't feel right. It didn't feel like the wind was on him anymore, but inside him. Tingles and aches ran through his body. Fear grew with the regret of ever following the smoky cloud. His body hurt, and he felt it changing. He squeezed his eyes shut.

The wind calmed and moved away from him and the pup as the ache faded. Austin lay panting on the ground. His breath felt different, and he tried to smack his lips, but that didn't work the same either. He opened his eyes and saw grey paws in front of him. The wolf pup pounced on Austin, his tail once again wagging.

You look just like me. Now we can play even better.

Austin's head snapped around, searching the clearing they'd been playing in for whoever just spoke.

Come on!

He looked at the pup. Austin realized it was the wolf pup who spoke to him. He said Austin looked just like him. He looked down to see fur covering his arms and hands. His fingers were bony toes with little claws. A longer neck allowed him to turn further sideways to see grey fur covering a body that wasn't his. Austin was a wolf.

With no other options, Austin followed the pup, stumbling over his feet, learning how to walk with paws for the first time. Once he gained control of his limbs, they wrestled, tumbled, and chased some more until they both lay down exhausted. After a rest, the pup stood.

Follow me. He took him into the trees, deeper into the woods. A shiver ran down Austin's spine. His fur moved, standing up on his back.

Two large adult wolves jumped out, cutting off the pup and Austin. Their eyes locked onto him, pinning him in place. Their lips pulled back and low growls emanated from their throats. Voices sounded through the air again.

You are not mine. It was the pup's mom. She stepped forward and grabbed the pup by the scruff and pulled him back. The other wolf, larger than the mom, paced toward Austin.

Go home. The echo of the voice was deep, similar to Austin's grandpa.

He's not a wolf. The pup wiggled out from behind his mom.

We know that. She tried to pull him back, but she missed and he bolted until he skidded to a stop before reaching Austin. The other wolf's lips pulled tight and the holes in his nose grew. Slim eyes snapped to attention and onto Austin.

Austin could feel his anger. He took a slow step back, knowing that whatever the wolf was about to do wouldn't be good.

But the smoky wind rushed out of nowhere and pushed the at the large wolf. The two adults huffed and growled low.

Fine. The word was a single deep rumble from the larger wolf. They left, and the wind hovered over Austin and the pup.

Come back to play. Okay?

Austin still wasn't sure how to respond, so he nodded. The wind nudged him away from the pup and the wolves and only stopped when they reached his clothes that lay in a bunch on the ground. The wind twirled around him, tingles and aches spread through his body. He tensed with the sensations, wishing they would go away. He tried to hold back his tears, but failed.

When the wind lifted away, Austin was himself again. He wiped at his wet cheeks and got dressed. He raced back through the woods to go home. As he approached the end of the trees and the top of the hill above his house, he heard his mom calling his name. Her voice pitched high with fear. He ran out of the trees yelling for her.

"Mom!"

"Austin?" She had been about to go back down the hill. She spun around. Austin ran and jumped as he reached her, leaving her to catch him. She stumbled back, but didn't fall. "There you are. You scared me!"

"I'm sorry, Mom." Austin's tears resurfaced. His mom held him while she started walking down the hill. When they reached the house, she set him down on the deck and wiped his eyes.

"Austin Zachary Hall, where were you and why did you

wander away?" He winced when she used his full name. His mom sounded calm, but Austin knew she wasn't. Something about the way she carefully said each word and how her breath pushed heavily out her nose.

"I chased a cloud of smoke and found a baby wolf."

"What?" His mom blinked, then shook her head. "Never mind. It's time for bed." She straightened and stretched out her arm with a pointed finger toward the door.

Bathed and dressed in pajamas, his mom tucked him into bed, then sat on the side.

"Austin, you know better than to run off like that." She paused. "Are you okay?" She ran her fingers over his forehead and pushed his hair back.

"I think so."

"Will you tell me what really happened?"

"I wasn't lying. I chased a cloud of smoke and found a baby wolf." Austin wanted her to believe that before he told her anything else. But by the look on her face, she didn't. She sighed.

"Okay, Austin. As long as you're okay. Get some sleep. I love you." She leaned down and kissed his forehead.

"I love you too, Mom."

Austin couldn't fall asleep. Kicking the blankets until they tangled at his feet, Austin sat up in bed and rested his chin on his hands and his elbows on his knees. He heard the phone ring and his mom answer.

"Hello. Oh, my goodness! Congratulations. A baby girl. I'm so happy for you two. What did you name her? Holly, what a beautiful name. I can't wait to tell Austin he has a new cousin."

EIGHT YEARS LATER...

AUSTIN LAY next to Holly in the field. The grass growing long toward the end of the summer hid them from sight of their parents.

"Why am I the only who calls you Zachary?" she asked.

Zachary was his middle name. She repeated it once as a toddler and it seemed to stick with her. She wasn't the only who called him Zachary, though.

"I don't know, Squirt."

"You're the only one who calls me Squirt."

"That's cause you are one." He nudged her with his elbow.

"Look! There's a lion. Do you see it?" Holly pointed her little finger up toward the sky at a rounded shaped cloud.

He didn't see a lion, but he wasn't about to admit that to Holly. "Yeah, I see it."

His cousin might be eight years younger than Austin, but they saw each other every day, and he loved her like a sister. But he feared that was about to change. Holly and her family were moving. Not that far that they'd never see each other again, but a town a few hours away. It wouldn't be the same not seeing Holly every day.

"I'm going to miss you, Squirt. Glad you didn't move before your birthday so I could still give you your gift."

"You never gave me a gift."

"I didn't?"

Holly giggled.

He reached into his front pocket and pulled out a necklace. He'd saved up from his job stocking shelves at the grocery store to buy this for her. It wasn't anything special, but it wasn't a cheap necklace that would tarnish or break as she wore it. Austin let it dangle from his fingers above her face. She gasped, and she sat up, gently taking the necklace from him. "Happy birthday, Holly."

She took her eyes off the necklace long enough to look down at him. "Thank you, Zachary."

Austin sat up and took the necklace from her to put it on. She lifted her hair. The necklace had a two-toned chain and a small heart locket. Inside he had *Love you, Squirt* engraved on one side and the other held a picture of the two of them from the beginning of summer. Holly opened the locket and ran a finger over the picture. She turned around.

"I love it." She launched herself upward and wrapped her arms around his neck. Even at eight years old, she was a tiny thing. She would be the tiniest one going into third grade at her new school. Without him around to protect her.

"Good." He pulled her off him and pinned her with a glare. "You remember everything I've taught you."

"I'll be fine, Zachary. My mom said she's sure everyone at my new school will be nice."

Yeah, sure they would. Austin didn't have much faith in other kids. Kids could be cruel at any age. Especially to someone as tiny as Holly.

"I love you."

"I love you too, Squirt."

"But I have to go now." She hugged him again and squeezed. He felt a single tear drop onto his shoulder. He held her tight, knowing he would miss hearing *Zachary* every day from her little voice. She was as close to a sister as he'd ever have.

The only brother he had was a wolf. Smoke was the grey pup he found in the woods the day Holly was born. Since being frightened by Smoke's parents, he never used his real name with the wolves. Smoke referred to him as Zachary, too. Now he understood it didn't matter what name he gave to wolves. But he liked that the special people in his life called him by a name no others did and few people knew.

"Let's go." Austin helped Holly up and took her hand to walk her home. She stopped and pulled on his arm.

"Did you see that?" She frowned at the trees up the hill. Austin looked, but saw nothing. He knew it wasn't Smoke. He could sense him if he was near.

"I don't see anything."

Holly still wouldn't move. "I know I saw something." She watched for another minute, then allowed Austin to pull her away.

He pulled her in for one last hug and kissed her forehead before letting her walk into her house, knowing she would leave in the morning before he'd see her again. He was saying goodbye to one of his best friends, his sister that wasn't really his sister.

CHAPTER 1

Zachary missed his motorcycle. Driving around this shit hole city in the same damn car as everyone else grated on his nerves. He drove the simple, small, grey SUV that appeared around every corner. He didn't want to stand out, and that was exactly what his motorcycle would do. And he hated it.

He'd been scouting out the address the woman, ghost, spirit, other being, whatever the hell she was, gave him. And he found nothing other than a building of offices. Each floor housed a different business. Insurance broker, realty agency, lawyer offices, and a public relations agency. When researching them, Zachary found well-built websites and contact information, but not much marketing. His attempts to contact each of them, posing as potential clients, only garnered recorded responses or automated messages. Access to the building was only granted with a passkey and no windows could open, were reinforced, and tinted.

The entire building was a front for something. But Zachary still didn't know what. The woman only gave him an address and a reassurance that Holly was mostly unharmed. *Mostly unharmed.* Those words ate at him with each day that passed, and he still hadn't found her. No sign whatsoever. But he'd been observing the patterns of the building.

Maybe she'd been wrong. If so, this had been a fucking waste of time. Time that he could have really used to find her.

Zachary drove to the campsite outside of town. He camped to make it easier to shift and to stay near Smoke, and he chose the side of town closest to where Holly was being held. Smoke stayed near the camp, but out of sight of the other campers. Zachary often went for *hikes* to shift and spend time with Smoke.

Zachary healed with Smoke by his side every day, but it wasn't the same for his wolf brother. Smoke still hurt from being abandoned by Zachary, even if that hadn't been his intention. Searching for Holly alone had been foolish and useless. And it had torn the two of them apart.

He arrived at camp and went in search of Smoke. Evening settled over the sky and the scent of the air changed with the coming of night. Campers were gathering around their fires, no longer wandering the trails. A couple hundred metres on the trail, Zachary veered off. He found the area Smoke claimed as a temporary territory. He moved around when he had to due to campers coming too close. Smoke hated it and told Zachary each day how much he missed Kai's pack. Zachary's jealousy grew, but he wasn't in the position to do anything. He had lost the right to feel this way.

Zachary ditched his clothes and hid them in a hole under a rock. A rock too heavy for most humans to move, but easy enough for a shifter. He shifted; the process beginning in his mind, then moved to his soul, pushing an ache through his body as each bone changed its position. Time as a wolf had been Zachary's escape from life while growing up. But it also came with its own challenges. He hadn't been treated any better by other wolves than he had by other humans.

He landed on the ground as the final waves of magic washed over him. Smoke emerged, dinner hanging from his jaws. He dropped the grouse in front of Zachary.

Still nothing? Smoke asked. They'd been there for almost three weeks and Zachary had yet to find a way into that building or confirm Holly was inside. Even a shifter's sense of smell couldn't penetrate the walls.

Nothing. Zachary had reached a dead end. So much rage and frustration filled his gut, but he refused to let it out. Because of Smoke. But some of Zachary's rage was directed at the death of Damien Marks. Zachary might have an address, but without Damien, he couldn't get inside.

How long are we going to stay here?

Smoke, if you want to go back to Kai's pack, then go. I can't force you to stay with me. Zachary snapped, some of his frustration leaking out. His tone filled with bitterness.

That isn't it. I'm with you. Smoke still hadn't lain down to eat the grouse. Zachary felt the strength of Smoke's eyes on him. *What you're doing isn't working. We need a different angle.*

You don't want to leave? Zachary had been sure he'd been miserable with him.

Smoke looked away and a long huff came out his nose. *I'm still hurt, and I know I shouldn't be. Not when I know how important Holly is to you. But it hurts just as much to be away from you. I'm with you. Brother.* Zachary's breath lurched as the word he'd needed most came from Smoke. Brother.

Maybe I need to get in touch with some contacts I'd rather avoid. See who took the place of Damien. It was the last thing he wanted to do.

Over the past month, Zachary had filled Smoke in on what he'd been doing for two years, how he'd finally found a trail and wormed his way into their circle enough to gain some trust. He'd been disgusted with himself anytime he stood next to Damien or anyone else inside that organization.

And Zachary had filled with remorse as Smoke told him of what he'd done for two years. Alone. Angry. Vicious. He'd become a whole different wolf. Zachary recognized how much he'd changed. And, Zachary thought, he had too.

I want to try for a little longer before contacting that group again. He hoped it never came to that.

Okay. After a firm nod, Smoke lay down to eat. Zachary followed, grateful to have his brother back, but the rift still needed to heal.

EZARAY HAD LOST count of the days after two years had passed. Her hope of ever escaping disappeared a long time ago. The only thing that kept her going was she knew this could be worse. Women were usually kidnapped for one purpose, and for the women here, that wasn't it. The women here needed to be kept healthy. She guessed they should be thankful for small miracles. They staffed the building with its own doctor and security. They let anyone caught treating the captives with anything worse than a shove *go*. All the women knew what they meant when they said *let go*. Let go meant someone was fired, but not here. Killed. They killed violators to let them go. Ezaray wasn't naïve. Not all women were in good standing here. If one lost too many times in a row, they disposed of them.

They had taken her and Holly on Holly's birthday. Holly had sensed them closing in, but she was too late. Ezaray knew she still blames herself for it every day, even though she stopped telling her.

Turning twenty had felt like such a big deal. Her life unfolding, and she'd been excited to dig in. Beginning a new job where she could grow and learn.

All that had happened. Just not the way she'd expected it would.

They hadn't gone to a club to drink, dance, and celebrate, but they had gone to the pub and stayed well into the night on their patio ordering appetizers and drinks. There had been four of them, Ezaray, Holly, and two other friends from high school. She didn't know what happened to them. They never saw them here. She grieved for her friends with the only assumption they had for what happened to them. But not long, and not often. There hadn't been the time when they worried about their own future.

Her handler kept her busy. For now, she and Holly had the same handler, but handlers changed. And when they did, they would set Ezaray against her best friend. It had happened before and would happen again. They traded and sold the women between handlers often. All part of their business.

The handlers watched for when they let each other win so as not to put their friend's life in danger, but rarely did they catch Holly pulling back. But that was because they didn't know Holly's true strength. She never allowed herself to show it. Holly had saved it for an escape someday, when she had still thought an escape was possible. To everyone else, Holly still seemed optimistic. Ezaray expected she put on an act, holding onto her hope solely to give to the other women and not for herself. That would be a Holly-like thing to do.

"Tallon, you fight tonight." Her handler appeared in their doorway, bedrooms disguised as offices. Gerard Young wasn't the worst handler in the company, but he only cared about the money and had no problem saying whatever to scare the shit out of Ezaray, Holly, or whoever else he controlled. The words worked on some of the newer girls.

"I thought Seely was fighting tonight." Ezaray learned to keep her voice small, compliant.

"She didn't make it." Gerard held a gravely joy in his one-sided sneer and a delightful spark in his eye. Ezaray refused to react, refused to swallow or allow her lips to twitch or her nostrils to flare, refused to allow Gerard to see a single tear fall with fear shining in the drop. She gave no reason for any handler to think her weak. She stared into his evil eyes for only a moment before she sat on her bed and pulled out her gear to prepare for the fight.

Gerard walked away, his slow footsteps fading. Holly emerged from the corner.

"Poor Kate." Her throat lodged on Kate's name. Kate had been trying hard for a long time, but as the days passed, her energy, her will to stay alive wavered. She'd lost her last fight. Holly knelt on the floor in front of Ezaray and helped her prepare. "Kate was supposed to fight Maggie tonight. Maggie's good, Zee." She didn't speak with awe of Maggie's skills, but fear that Ezaray's didn't match hers.

"I'll be fine, Holly." Her grief over Kate kept her voice flat. Empty words were the norm when trying to encourage Holly. They both knew the truth of their situation. She kept the words, but let go of the hope.

Holly and Ezaray were two of the best fighters in the company, but so was Maggie.

In her shorts and sports bra and with her hands wrapped, Ezaray ran through some warm-ups and drills with Holly while waiting for Gerard to tell her it was time to go.

THE RAIN WOULD PROVIDE AN EXCUSE. As long as Zachary's acting skills were up to par. He stalked the alleys, waiting for the *well-dressed men* to enter the building. The apparent business hours were erratic. Zachary tracked movement for a pattern, but the people coming and going weren't consistent. He familiarized himself with recurring scents and features. The pattern may not be consistent, but the clientele was.

He'd studied each man that walked into the building for the past two weeks. He knew who the difficult targets would be by their arrogant struts and high chins. And he recognized the weak and new clients by how their eyes searched the area as they approached the building and again before they opened the door. Their gait was slower than others, and their posture didn't carry the straight sharpness that increased their height and changed the air surrounding them. These were the easy targets, the ones he intended to con.

Zachary had gone shopping earlier in the day, to dress to match others. Button-up dress shirts and slacks. Sweaters and sweater vests adorned some older patrons, but Zachary would never touch them. The dress code of business casual matched the businesses labelled in white decals on the glass of the front door.

He yanked off the tag on the sleeve of the navy blue button-up shirt and rolled up the cuffs. Sinking his body against the building across the street to hide himself in shadows, he watched the door and the men that approached, waiting for the right moment, the right target.

And there he was. Short, young, and grew up with money and privilege. He wore tailored clothes, but he'd yet to grow into the broader shoulders of his frame. He walked with self-assurance until he got closer to the building. His steps faltered and his head turned from side to side with the smallest movements.

The street emptied, the crowd entering slowed for the moment. Zachary dashed from the alley, the rain sticking his shirt to his chest and back.

The grey wind quickly blew through the street as he crossed. He watched it disappear, knowing it meant something important, but he refused to get distracted.

"Hold the door!" he boomed through the rain the moment the guy ran his passkey over the box outside the door. Zachary grabbed the frame above his head and shook out his hair. In his other hand he held a blank white card. It did nothing and didn't hold the same luster as the passkeys he'd seen people use, but in the dimness of the rainy evening, it passed inspection for any cameras and the young guy in front of him.

Zachary glared down at him and watched him visibly swallow. He took one step to face Zachary.

"In." He gestured with his hand enough that the guy noticed the white card between his fingers. The guy moved and Zachary followed, keeping his eyes forward and using his sense of smell to track his surroundings.

The inside looked like any other high-end business. Plush waiting areas sat on each side of the door, their fabric without a single dent, rip or stain. A man in his sixties with a blue security uniform sat behind the main desk staring at computer monitors. Zachary wondered if his job was just for show. A place running an illegal business should have better security than him.

And they did.

That security stood in the form of a man larger than Zachary next to the elevators at the end of the lobby. He blocked one boarded up elevator entrance. The other elevator had the same electronic box on the outside to call it.

Zachary stayed behind the smaller man — kid, he was barely a man — and kept his card in his hand. The box beeped as the kid ran his key over it. The security guy eyed him, then Zachary. Zachary returned his glare and nodded, lifting his hand so he saw his card. The guy hesitated, but the elevator opened and Zachary moved in beside the kid before he could say anything. He'd gotten lucky with his timing. Getting in shouldn't have been that easy.

The elevator had one direction — down. He'd be trapped underground. His muscles tensed as he prepared himself the best he could. The kid watched Zachary with the side of his eye. He quickly turned his head away when Zachary glared at him. Zachary's lips twitched as he smelled fear spike for a moment from the kid. He was easy to intimidate. The problem was, even Zachary was feeling a bit intimidated by his situation. There'd be no way out if he were caught.

Zachary's senses ran wild when the doors opened. He stepped out of the elevator without anyone stopping him. At first glance, the room looked to be a gentlemen's club. Cigar smoke floated around the air. Glass tumblers of amber liquid were in the hands of most of the men. A shiny, dark stained, wooden bar ran along one entire wall with five male bartenders behind it. Security guards similar to the one on the floor above roamed. Booths, tall tables, and end tables with plush furniture circled the room. But what stood out amongst it all, out of place for a gentleman's club, was the fighting ring in the centre.

Whatever he just walked into started a sickness in his gut that tried to eat its way out with a burning sensation.

The kid walked off, joining a group his own age that greeted him with cheers. Zachary ambled over to the bar, watching the other customers to see what they required when ordering a drink. Simple cash. Green twenties passed from the customers to the bartender.

A lanky bartender, white shirt, black vest, stood across from him with a raised brow, until his eyes met Zachary's dark scowl. The man flinched and stepped back half a step.

"Whiskey." Zachary pulled out a twenty he had tucked beside his wallet and passed it over. Seconds later, the bartender set his glass in front of him and moved on to the next guy, but not before sending a wary look at Zachary. In a place like this, he welcomed the reaction.

Two chairs and a small table sat empty in a darker alcove. Zachary made his way over and sat to observe the room. Without knowing the purpose of this place, he didn't want to talk to anyone and make it known he didn't belong.

The scents were strong and plenty. Several flavours of cigars and cologne mingled together. Strong amber alcohols filled most glasses. And the distinct scent of cash wafted here and there. Men of all ages, but all wealthy, stood in groups, a few meandering with social delight.

After half an hour, a clearing of a throat echoed through unseen speakers. Attention turned toward the ring. A man dressed in a black suit stood in the centre, smiling at the room, his white teeth showing beneath his shaped, dark facial hair. A ponytail pulled his hair tightly away from his face.

"Welcome, gentlemen." He held a microphone in one hand. The club took up the entire basement space of the building. "Tonight's event promises to be a good one. Our girls will come around shortly to collect your bets. A reminder, the minimum bet is five thousand dollars. If you're new or have yet to get to know some of our girls, do so this evening. Find your favourite and invest in their future." Excitement rose in his voice as he spread his arm outward to encompass the club. His eyes were wide and focused above a grin meant to seduce the men to spend their money.

Excited faces donned many of them, and their eyes often looked toward the back of the room. Zachary kept himself seated. After ten minutes, an elevator dinged in the distance and the atmosphere of the murmurs changed.

Female scents filtered through the crowd. Their anxiety-tinged aromas soured his nose. The well-groomed centre man implied the girls were here of their own free will, choosing this to make a life for themselves. They weren't and every person in this room knew it.

The men parted, giving Zachary glimpses of the girls making their way through the crowd individually. All wearing short spandex shorts and sports bras and carrying tablets with an electronic tap to record bets and accept money. A redhead waded through the men, but she wasn't carrying a tablet like the rest. Fabric wrapped her hands, as if ready for a boxing match. The fighting ring was for the girls. If there was one fighter, then there was another floating through the crowd.

Zachary had to force his breathing to create a steady

pace when his body would rather rush air in and out of him like the quick motions of a saw.

A scent that smelled like home, like sweet wildflowers and fresh summer grass, crossed his nose and grew stronger. He only recognized her by her picture. She turned into a beautiful full-grown version of the little girl he played with every day since the day she was born, since the day he became a shifter.

"Hey, Squirt." He didn't raise his voice for fear of others hearing him, and he hoped Holly heard him as she passed. Her sharp intake hit his ears, and she turned around. Wide green eyes locked onto him, hurting him in a way he didn't think possible.

"Zachary?" She whispered his name and her eyes filled with moisture. Holly plastered a seductive smirk on her lips and turned toward him. One step and Zachary flinched. She halted. She wasn't the same Holly he used to know. All the wildflowers and summer grass were drowned out by a distinct wild scent of an owl. Holly's seductive look wavered, but she recovered.

"Wolf." The look on her face was inviting, but her snub wasn't.

"Owl." He wasn't as shocked to meet another shifter as she seemed to be.

"What the hell are you doing here?" Accusation leached from her lips that barely moved with her whisper. She didn't have to speak up for him to hear her and vice versa.

"Looking for you."

"You're not..." She swallowed before she tried again. "You're not here for the events?"

"No, I'm not."

Holly's chin quivered.

"Don't cry, Squirt. We need to get you out of here before you can cry."

"You can't. There's no way out, Zachary." Harshness edged each word. Holly was desolate and her eyes were shells of the little sister he missed having around and last saw so many years ago.

Another girl, similar features and size to Holly's still petite frame, sidled up next to her. Zachary's eyes blinked rapidly, and an involuntary growl reverberated through his body. It was a damn good thing he was already sitting or the dizziness and headache would have put him on his ass. She had a scent full of sweet cherries and he wanted to devour her.

Hell of a place to discover his mate.

His focus blurred, but he heard Holly, her words thick like spoken over a swollen tongue muffled in his ears.

"Are you okay?"

"I'm sure he's fine. There's more that would like to place bets." Her melodic inflection cut through the haze, trying to urge Holly to move on.

"Don't leave." His growl tore at his throat.

"What is it, Zachary?" Holly reached for him, but pulled her hand back.

"You know him? Wait. Zachary. That Zachary?"

"Yeah."

Zachary focused his eyes on his mate and as soon as he did, his gut sank to the floor. Her hands didn't hold a tablet like the rest. They were wrapped and ready to fight. Both still stood with practiced seduction and flirtatious expressions, never breaking from their act. No one looking on would think they were having any discussion other than his interest in a fighter.

She was the reverse image of Holly. Her dark hair was

pulled tight into two braids exposing the creamy column of her neck. His eyes roamed down her body noting her curves, that he imagined were slimmer than normal, left bare from her outfit.

"What's your name?"

"Fighter names only. Tallon."

Zachary turned his eyes to Holly, demanding with a look she tell him her name.

"Ezaray," she whispered.

"Holly," Ezaray admonished.

"It doesn't matter, Zee. He's leaving." She pinned her eyes on him. Long gone was the little girl. "And he's never coming back here." In her place stood a pint-sized shifter. She marched off for two steps, then corrected the sway of her hips before she sidled up to another group of men.

Ezaray hesitated in front of him.

"Can I touch you?"

"It's not against the rules, but you can't hurt me."

"Never." He waited for her to step closer, then he stood. He caught her leaning into him as he towered over her. His hand lifted and ran down her arm, feeling the muscle beneath her pale skin. With the heat that ignited from his touch, his weakness grew and he had to sit back down.

He was eye level to her wrapped hands. His veins throbbed with the quick rage of rushing blood. It didn't matter how many times he'd been exposed to violence, even violence worse than this. All he wanted was to tear the throats out of every man in here.

"You fight well?" Zachary wished he sounded smoother as he saw Ezaray flinch when he spoke.

"Yeah, I do."

"What happens if you lose?"

"Depends how often I lose."

"You going to win tonight?" He tried to instil confidence and encouragement.

"Probably not." Ezaray backed away, her eyes lost in his, before she turned away into the crowd.

Zachary had to watch his mate fight. A fight that could be for her life.

CHAPTER 2

Ezaray had been right about Holly's hope vanishing. Even with the sight of her childhood hero, Zachary, no fresh spark ignited. Holly believed this was their future, their life. She no longer looked for a way out, even if that possibility showed up in the form of a rescuer.

Ezaray didn't know if Holly was right. Didn't know what she believed herself. But something pulled her toward Zachary. For him to be here was risky. Even more so that he knew who they were.

The first steps she took to walk away from him were difficult. Her feet buried into the floor in front of him. His touch had changed something within her.

An ache began as she walked away, and it took considerable effort not to turn around to look at him. She needed to concentrate. Her chances of beating Maggie were slim. She couldn't afford a distraction. A distraction that was a dream and nothing more. A dream that couldn't exist. All a dream like that would do is cause pain and depression.

Ezaray worried for Holly. Unsure what would happen to her mind if they kept her here much longer.

The look on Ezaray's face was practiced, as was the sway of her hips when she walked through the room. Her thoughts never in the moment. But she always looked the part of an alluring fighter, and many of the men spent their money based on the look of the girl rather than their skill. Sly eyes and sexy smirks were her answer to most men's questions. She didn't need words. None of them did when it was their fight night. The girls taking the bets gave the fighter statistics.

The adrenaline in her blood pumped harder the further around the room she walked. The fight didn't happen right away. They gave the crowd time to get excited. Once the girls all circled the room, the fighters prepped in the back and the rest went to a balcony viewing area reserved for them.

Ezaray and Maggie separated from the rest of the girls.

"Good luck, Zee," Holly whispered and nodded to Maggie. "You too, Maggie." Ezaray softened her features toward the other fighter, but Maggie said nothing. She kept to herself, never getting to know the rest of them. She could be worse. A few of the girls were nasty, expecting the hateful attitude would put them on top and secure their safety. Handlers didn't care how a fighter acted with the other girls, as long as their fighters didn't get hurt in a way that incapacitated them. If they couldn't fight, they couldn't make money. And the only rule during a fight was no permanent damage to your opponent. Getting severely hurt during a fight was acceptable. It brought in more money, more bets during the fight, increased crowds at the next event.

Maggie sat on a bench, her eyes glued to the floor between her legs, her knees bouncing up and down. Ezaray didn't have much of a pre-fight routine. She took deep breaths while she stretched her muscles, preparing her body the best she could. She straightened the wraps on her hands, ensuring they were in place and secure. Then she waited, her eyes glued to the door for Gerard and Maggie's handler to barge through with eager grins and bulged pants.

Her thoughts drifted to Zachary. She'd heard so many stories of him from Holly growing up. For years, she'd thought Holly had had a crush on him, the way her eyes sparked when she talked of him, but she'd learned over time that he was actually Holly's cousin and she thought of him as her brother, a misunderstood hero with a heart of gold that she'd looked up to.

Ezaray would have thought the sight of her childhood hero would have started an infinitesimal light of hope in Holly's chest, but her dismissive demeanour showed her soul was dormant. But Zachary's silver eyes lit the tiniest fire in the back of Ezaray's mind. That little light was hope. It would be foolish to allow it to grow or gain any strength.

Despite knowing the door would open, the bang of it against the wall made both her and Maggie jump. Gerard stood there with his arm outstretched, holding the door while Dagon, Maggie's handler, towered behind him.

"Time to fight, girls." Each word rolled through her ears like boiling bile. Eyes straight ahead, Ezaray walked out the door past the handlers with Maggie following behind. The cheers began through the crowd as each man saw them appear. She saw the rest of the girls sitting in their seats from her peripheral vision, fear shining behind their eyes despite whatever outward emotion they showed toward each other.

Chin high, she walked to the ring and stepped up the carpeted stairs. Pulling the top rope up, she bent to climb through and settled in one corner, leaning against the post. Ezaray slowly checked in with each muscle in her body, preparing herself to do her best, but also facing the reality that she would get hurt tonight.

With his quiet steps and cocksure stride, Tyrone made his way to the centre of the ring with his microphone in hand. He owned the building, owned the business, and as he ensured every handler knew, he ultimately owned the girls.

As soon as they take a girl and add her to the group of fighters, they first meet with Tyrone. Ezaray couldn't forget the day they threw her and Holly into his office. Holly had spat in his face and Ezaray had refused to speak. Tyrone didn't break girls by beating them or starving them. He threw them into their first fight with the best of the fighters. They weren't given a choice but to comply. He made it clear, if they lost too many fights, they lost their value. He disposed of useless items.

Some girls had tried to gain favour with Tyrone, offering themselves to pull them above others and give them a chance to get outside of the building, to escape. But Tyrone never laid a hand on any of the girls. That scared Ezaray the most about him.

"Time for the main event, gentlemen. I hope you've placed all your bets. Tallon versus Martin is a close match and won't disappoint, I guarantee." He paused, pulling the attention of each man in the room as his smile grew while he turned in a circle. "They fight!" He roared, a sound echoed by the crowd.

The ding that sounded throughout her nightmares chimed and Ezaray and Maggie stepped forward, hands up, bouncing on their feet. It snuffed out the little light of hope ignited by Zachary. She didn't want to lose tonight, but neither did she want to win. There was no winning left in her future.

ZACHARY'S STOMACH lurched as his mate stepped into the ring. Violent claws tore at his insides, urging him to shift and hurt every male in this room, but his weakened body at the first scent of his mate flattened him to the chair. There was nothing he could do but watch her fight, watch her get hurt.

The bell rang and Ezaray and the other fighter moved from their corners, both light on their feet, hands up, muscles loose, and eyes focused. Ezaray didn't strike first, keeping herself on the defensive from the beginning.

He knew his body was too weak to do anything, yet his muscles tensed and his feet were firmly planted on the floor, ready to take on every man in here for using women the way they do.

She blocked and dodged expertly until she didn't, swaying with the blow of the other fighter's fist against her jaw. Her foot stepped back to keep her from falling and her hand went up to block the next attack. While hunched over, she clenched her fist and angled her wrist. She twisted while she straightened and returned the punch. Pride-filled adrenaline spiked in his blood as the other fighter stumbled from Ezaray's strike. More blocks and hits from both girls and the crowd turned restless. They were too evenly matched.

The men wanted more, and Zachary fought the urge to snarl.

Movement to his side caught his attention. Someone sat in the chair on the other side of the small round table. Silk button-up shirt and a tumbler in his hand. His scent rose and Zachary flinched with a growl.

"Easy, wolf." The shifter's calm, condescending baritone

pissed Zachary off. Zachary inhaled, the shifter's scent familiar.

"Hawk. I've seen you before." Perched on a branch above Asher's headquarters he was building near his pair's pack.

"And I you. I've observed your little gang a few times." He lifted his glass to his lips and sipped while he watched the fight, his interest not appearing to be on Zachary.

"Rude of you not to introduce yourself," he quipped.

"I'm not sure how you got in here. But I must ask why you're here."

"Now, I don't see that as any of your business. But I would like to ask you the same question. What's your role in a place like this?" Any ally on the inside of this place would be a blessing, but a shifter that was an enemy could kill them all.

"Since I know you and your friends are a group of good ole boys, I can share. I'm not here for the reasons any in the room believe. Your turn."

"Looking for someone." With his minimal strength, his tone was short, but he didn't want to share with this strange shifter until he knew him better.

The hawk shifter's hand lifted and rested on the small table. After a few moments, he set it back in his lap. "For proper access." A white nondescript card lay on the table. "See you around, wolf." He rose and wandered through the room, his eyes on the fight.

Zachary seemed to have an ally in the hawk. But appearances could deceive.

He put his control to the test more than ever before as he watched his mate weaken with each hit from the other fighter. His body weakened further as he fought with himself to stay still, to douse all reactions, to keep his hands from breaking the arm of the chair or the glass in his hand.

Rage and pain had their own fighting match in his chest as he felt every blow his mate took.

Holly's desolation made sense to him, now. There was nothing he could do. At least not yet. He didn't understand how they managed this place. But he'd been given that opportunity, thanks to the hawk shifter.

Ezaray's knees hit the floor. Zachary forced his eyes shut as he felt them heat with the flash of a wolf. When he opened them a moment later, he caught Holly looking at him from the balcony. Her eyes glowed an interesting shade of orange, but with an imperceptible shake, they returned to normal.

Holly hadn't been a shifter the day she moved away from Hull Creek. Even from Holly, Zachary had hidden that part of himself. If he were to tell anyone, it would have been her, but he'd believed she was still too young to keep that kind of secret for someone else. He should have done better to keep in touch with her as the years passed. Maybe he could have helped her through so many things. Maybe he would have been around when she'd been taken and rescued her sooner. But how would he have discovered his mate? Fate had a design for the things She controlled, and Zachary believed it was sometimes an evil one.

TEARS CLOGGED HER EYES. No matter how much she wanted to cry, her body wasn't capable. Through one eye that was quickly swelling, Ezaray looked to where Zachary was sitting. His eyes glued to Holly across the room. There was nothing there for her. He came here for Holly and no one else.

She tilted her head so Maggie could see her lips and she

mouthed the words she was always too stubborn to say. *Just knock me out.* There were only two ways a fight could end. The moment before debilitating damage could be done to a fighter or a fighter getting knocked unconscious. Ezaray hated that moment of oblivion, but after seeing a spark of hope taken away, and against Maggie, she craved the moment like a sexy dream.

I can't, Maggie mouthed back. They both knew Ezaray could fight longer, and if anyone caught onto the quick knockout, they'd both be in trouble.

Maggie waited for Ezaray to get up. With only herself to rely on, she pulled together strength she knew she had at one point. Imagining this was one of her early fights when she had the determination to succeed and not only fear for her safety. The thoughts created a placebo effect for strength, but if it got her on her feet, she didn't care.

Ezaray managed several more hits of her own. Maggie wasn't in the best shape, but she was better off than Ezaray. The strength left her arms, and they dropped just enough for Maggie to use a final blow to knock her out.

Finally, she could sleep.

Or not.

She came to with faces above her. The doctor's and Gerard's. Cheers erupted throughout the room. She blinked and looked past the doctor and her handler to see Maggie with her arm held in the air by Dagon.

"That wasn't close enough, Tallon. You could have done better than that." Gerard's disgust spat from his mouth, hitting her already sweaty and blood-covered face. At the moment, Ezaray didn't care, but she knew she would later. She would worry about her status and track her statistics for the likelihood of becoming trash.

The doctor's hazel eyes bore into hers before he nodded

and helped her sit up with gentle hands around her shoulders.

"Gentlemen, show Tallon some encouragement. She'll need it for their rematch next season." Tyrone lazed against a post inside the ring. He crossed his arms and his narrowed eyes studied both fighters. The men gave an applause and a few cheers. Not enough to lift the spirits of a professional fighter, let alone a captive one.

After Maggie's handler released her wrist, the doctor led both girls out of the ring and through the crowd to the back room. The doctor was an enigma. Not a single fighter could read him. Holly herself never had an opinion. Not one she shared.

He treated Ezaray first. He patted the table, and she dutifully climbed up.

"Pay no attention to Gerard, Tallon. You fought well." The doctor's clipped tone had an odd calming cadence. He worked on cleaning the cuts on her face. She wouldn't believe any man involved in this business would be kind, but he was as close as any of them came. His eyes darted behind him. "As did you, Martin."

He was good at his job. Part of the image of this place was the beauty of the fighters. Keeping them free of scars and other permanent damage was his responsibility. And no fighter fought again until they had fully healed. Appearance brought in more money. Tyrone and the handlers wouldn't accept anything less.

The doctor, he had no other name around here, finished tending her face and checked over the rest of her. He gave her the same specific instructions he did after every fight, and Ezaray nodded along as she always did. Until he gripped her chin in his fingers.

"You will listen."

"Understood." Why did he care?

Ezaray slid off the table and traded places with Maggie. The doctor tended her with the same care he showed Ezaray, also enforcing his order when she nodded along with disinterest.

He ushered them back to their rooms and informed each of them he would be back to check on them soon. Ezaray collapsed on her bed. Holly wouldn't return until the end of the night. Those that weren't fighting sometimes acted as servers for the guests, building interest in themselves.

She understood why many girls gave up, stopped winning fights, and attempted to harm themselves. Ezaray was too stubborn for that, but she understood why they did it. This wasn't a good life. It wasn't a fair life. That weighed on her mind often. The abuse they suffered was unorthodox. Emotionally, yes, but physically, they were kept in great health. But they were used. Imprisoned and used as puppets. They had been turned into something they weren't. Not a girl brought in yet had been a true fighter. Those that learned and adapted stayed the longest.

After every fight, Ezaray wondered if her stubbornness would ever wear out.

Tonight differed from most nights. The appearance of Zachary threw her off. She wanted to talk to Holly about him. But none of it mattered. They'd never see him again.

CHAPTER 3

E zaray and the other fighter had disappeared, not returning to the floor with the rest of the girls. Holly avoided his gaze. He had so many questions, but couldn't get any answers if she wouldn't talk to him.

What surprised Zachary the most was the doctor that appeared in the ring after the redhead knocked out Ezaray. The hawk shifter bent over Zachary's mate to examine her. To watch another shifter touch his mate when he couldn't was torture. To keep his composure was worse.

Heat ran through his veins and his skin crawled as he forced himself to stay still. Zachary choked down his growl, a growl that if let loose would echo out of the alcove.

He stayed where he was, nursing his drink for another hour until the hawk shifter walked by. He paused.

"You're still here."

"Good eyes." Zachary wouldn't admit to him his body was still too weak to move. Although, he hadn't tried. He couldn't stand the thought of having to leave Holly after he'd finally found her. And now, he was forced to leave his mate in the same place. "So, you're a doctor."

"What are you here for?"

Zachary glared up at the other shifter. He wasn't about to answer any questions to a member of this organization, even one that claimed he wasn't evil.

"Fine, don't tell me, but I can guess. The girls are fine. And you should leave."

Zachary acknowledged him with a nod, dismissing him so he didn't have an audience when he attempted to move. Bracing himself, he stood. And just in time. His hand snaked out and gripped Holly's elbow.

"Let go, Zachary. You shouldn't be here."

"I came for you, Squirt. I will get you out. And Ezaray. She a friend of yours?"

"Best friend. Since I moved away from Hull Creek. You need to forget about both of us."

"Can't happen." He spoke with the same authority he used on her as kids. It had worked then, but something told him it wouldn't work now.

She might have had a smile on her face when she tore her arm from his grasp, but there was nothing left in her empty eyes.

Zachary resigned himself to leave them here, knowing there was no way to get them out tonight. The hawk had given him the opportunity to study this place. To get them out.

He left, needing to regain his strength after meeting his mate for the first time before he drew unwanted attention. Leaving the same way he came in, he passed the same security guards. All eyed him with the same suspicion, but Zachary didn't give them a second glance. He walked out into the rain, carrying the confidence with which he'd walked in there.

The rain soaked through his clothes, but he felt none of

it. He shook out his hair before he got into the rental car. The seats were soaked from his clothes only seconds after he got behind the wheel. Arriving at his campsite, he found Smoke hiding in the bushes. He threw his clothes over a tree branch and shifted.

I found her. And I found my mate.

Then where are they? Smoke sniffed the air and looked behind Zachary.

It won't be easy to get them out. I need to learn how they manage the place first. Holly doesn't think it's possible and has no hope of it. Oh, and Holly's a shifter. An owl.

Really? Excitement pitched inside Smoke, and Zachary caught a sense of the playful pup he used to be. He'd always wanted to meet Holly, but Zachary wouldn't let him.

Yup. And there's another shifter inside too. The company doctor.

Is he friend or foe? Smoke quickly turned serious.

I don't know yet. But he gave me a real passkey for the place. I can walk in and out of there without security stopping me. There must have been something in his tone that made Smoke narrow his eyes.

What is that place?

Zachary told him. He told him everything. Not since before they were separated had Zachary been that open with Smoke. He'd never been that vulnerable before. Zachary had to go back, but a mass of terror dropped in his stomach at the thought of the weakness that overcame him and in a place so dangerous. Weakened, he wouldn't be able to protect Holly or his mate.

Zachary thought back on everything Asher explained about how he'd found Gwen. He hadn't mated her right away. He'd spent time with her and eventually the weakness faded, as long as he continued to see her. If he didn't go back for them, he'd end up like Nathan stuck in a painful, shifted state, roaming around as an angry wolf.

He'd integrated himself into Damien's business to discover where Holly was. He could do the same now to get Holly and Ezaray out. And he needed to do it alone.

THE DOCTOR SAT on the side of Ezaray's bed, hovering over her. His fingers warm and gentle, rubbing ointment over the cuts on her face. He'd been in to see her and Maggie at least twice a day. How none of them ever scarred, Ezaray didn't know. Many thought the doctor was magic. Magic hands or his ointments were magic potions, she didn't care. Whatever kept them alive. Not even a week later and their cuts were healing better than normal. They always did.

"Do you have any other health concerns?" He asked with each visit, and he always insisted they tell him the truth. She didn't know if anyone ever did, but Ezaray didn't. He might seem kind, but he worked for Tyrone. She'd never give them a reason to get rid of her. Thankfully, she stayed healthy.

"No."

He nodded. "You're healing well. So is Maggie." In private, the doctor used their real first names rather than the fake personas given by Tyrone. His mouth opened, then his face tightened. He looked like he wanted to say more, he always did, but he sealed his lips and put his things away. He stood, giving Ezaray space to sit up on her bed. "I'll be back tonight."

The doctor looked across the room at Holly. Ezaray watched her chin lift and she met his eyes. The doctor exhaled then left, shutting their door quietly behind him, too quiet. Holly huffed and squished her pillow further into her lap.

Holly had turned agitated since the night of the fight, and it bothered Ezaray that she wouldn't talk to her. Zachary. Maybe Holly wasn't as unaffected by his appearance as she let on.

Since losing the fight to Maggie, Ezaray's despair increased. There would be a rematch in a few months. Her chances of winning that one would be about the same as the last.

"What is it about the doctor that makes you challenge him like that? He's the only man in this place that you'll look in the eye."

"There's nothing." Holly shut down her question like she always did. "I don't challenge him. I'm hungry. Let's go."

Holly stood and only waited for Ezaray once she reached their bedroom door. They walked through the halls of the office, past other rooms. The main lobby of this floor had been turned into a kitchen and lounge. The girls had access to the entire floor, but security was always thick. They stocked the kitchen well, and the girls made their own meals. And they expected them to eat. If they didn't, Tyrone stood watch while his security guards force fed them. Ezaray had seen it happen only once. Whether or not she was hungry, she ate three full meals a day.

Ezaray and Holly worked together to make themselves something to eat while the rest of the girls trickled in. Maggie walked in alone, her arms crossed and her eyes down. The red cuts on her face were healing marks of pink and the bruises were fading into yellow. Fresh ointment shone under the fluorescent lights. The doctor must have just left her.

As the room filled, Ezaray took out more ingredients to add to what they were making. Might as well try to feed everyone, but as she set the containers on the counter, Carmen stomped over.

"Don't touch all the food. I can make my own and so can everyone else. As long as you two hurry."

Ezaray sent an apologetic look toward some of the other girls. Carmen was one of the few that felt they needed to compete and treated them like the enemies rather than the men surrounding them. Ezaray used to feel sorry for her, but even after being friendly, she still treated them all like shit. Carmen was on her own. Well, her and her two cronies, Tina and Rachel. They were the type that tried to sleep with Tyrone, the handlers, the security. Anyone they thought could help them rise in the ranks. Anything to be treated like royalty in this building or give them a chance to escape. This place didn't work like that. The only way they valued you was if you won every single fight. And even that was never a guarantee.

She closed the containers and set them back in the fridge. Moving to the other side of the stove, she helped Holly and made space for someone else to start their own meal. The smug look on Carmen's face as she moved in pissed Ezaray off, but she let it go. Holly muttered something under her breath, but she didn't hear it. She was sure it was a choice name for Carmen. Probably rhymed with itch.

They sat around the table in various stages of their meals. Security hovered. Carmen set her plate on the table at the same time Ezaray pushed hers away.

"You worried now?" The twitch of Carmen's lips told her she hoped Ezaray was worried.

"Why would I be?" It would have been better not saying anything, but Ezaray wasn't in the mood to be quiet.

"You lost. It wasn't your first loss either. I wouldn't be surprised if you go on the watch list." Carmen wasn't all wrong. It hadn't been her first loss, but she wasn't in danger of being on the watch list. Yet. If they kept matching her with Maggie, or even Holly, she would be in danger.

"I'm not worried. I beat you two fights in a row. I'm not the one at the top of their watch list." Ezaray would never add to another's fear for their life, except Carmen's. Carmen did it to every single girl here, even her little followers. She no longer got any sympathy.

"Watch it, Tallon. Gerard's been sniffing out other girls. We might be bunk mates." The threat in her eyes drowned her cheery words. Ezaray didn't know if what she'd said about Gerard was true, but it wasn't anything she needed to worry about. Handlers traded all the time. That wasn't anything new. Living with Carmen would be a pain in the ass, though.

HE COULD FEEL Smoke's eyes on his back as he walked away from camp to go to the club. Smoke's worry was thick, and it stabbed Zachary with both guilt and warmth. Guilt over their lost years and warmth to know he still cared. They were still a pair, still bonded.

Zachary got in his car and drove into town. When scouting the place, it seemed busiest on Thursdays. Sparks ran through his veins. Just the thought of seeing his mate revved his system into overdrive. His senses fired, but his limbs turned weak. He'd never be able to save them if he couldn't regain his strength when he was around his mate.

He ran the passkey over the black box outside the doors. His breath stuck in his throat until the light turned green and he heard the lock disengage. Zachary still didn't know if he should trust the hawk, but he got through the first door.

The older blue suit security guard sat barely awake behind the desk, but the larger black suit by the elevator narrowed focused eyes on him as he approached. Zachary ran his passkey over the box by the elevator and the doors dinged as they opened. The guy turned his attention back to the front of the lobby.

He let out an inaudible sigh. Zachary rode the elevator alone. With his eyes closed, he braced himself for whatever he'd see on the other side of the doors. He hated how he fit into a place like this, how he'd fit in with Damien's organization. This wasn't who he really was, but this was how people saw him. He'd fought against people's, and wolves', perception of him. Until one day. Not long after Holly had moved away from Hull Creek. He still wasn't the bad boy people thought he was, but he hung out with the wrong people, made some bad decisions, picked some fights just for the hell of it. He might look at home in a place like this, but he didn't really belong. There wasn't anywhere he belonged.

Until he found Asher. He remembered finding Gwen in Hull Creek, looking for him as it turned out. Smoke had attacked Asher's pair and despite that, they took him in. Then they began a search for Zachary.

Gwen had smelled different, like a shifter, but lacking something. The scent that stood out the most on her was Smoke's. He'd followed her back to Alder Ridge and confronted both of them.

Asher's little shifter pack felt like home. And he had to push them away for this. He'd never forgive himself if they got hurt trying to help him. Smoke would never forgive him.

He wanted that home intact when they returned. When they returned with Holly and Ezaray.

He raised his eyelids as the doors opened and kept his breaths shallow, taking in the scents of the room slowly. He walked to the bar and ordered a whiskey. It would take too much of the alcohol to affect him, but he'd grown to like the taste of it over the years.

Zachary surveyed the room and ambled around the outer edge. He'd only seen one side last time. Now, he walked to see the full layout. The sides were identical except for the bar, and the back and front each had elevators and a door that led to the stairs. Security guards blocked the doors to the stairs and the back elevator. There was one other door in the back corner, also guarded. Peering past the guard, Zachary saw a hall through the small window.

A raised viewing box sat near the ring on the opposite side. The girls who weren't fighting sat there last time. Forced to watch each other fight, watch each other lose.

He cautiously allowed his senses to reach further. Inhaling, he didn't smell his mate, or Holly. He focused on the scent of a hawk and couldn't smell him either. Zachary had arrived earlier than last time, but the lower numbers still surprised him based on what he'd seen when watching the place. He made his way around the room and back to the bar. He counted each security guard he could find, noted their size and the weapons he could detect on each.

At the bar, he ordered another whiskey and made his way to the same seat he'd taken before. He waited for something to happen.

After half an hour of being disgusted with the sight of the men in the room, waiting to watch innocent women fight for entertainment, forced into this life, he finally smelled the hawk.

"Have any trouble getting in the building?" The shifter sat down beside him and lifted his glass to his lips.

"None. Should I have?" Zachary's mistrust came through his tone. Asher and Gwen had been the first people he'd trusted with ease. A doctor in a place like this didn't fall into the same category as them.

"No. But you'll be noticed if you come often." Zachary narrowed his eyes at the hawk. "If they figure out you're not meant to be here and didn't go through the vetting process, we'll both be killed. You first, me later when they figure out I helped you get in."

"What's your role here? Why should I trust you?"

"I'm not the bad guy. I'm not one of them." Zachary felt the anger that rolled through the hawk.

"I need more than that."

The hawk sighed, his body relaxing again. "I'll meet you at your campsite tonight when I'm finished here." He stood without looking at Zachary and left toward the back of the room. Zachary watched him disappear near the corner of the door that led to the hall.

If the hawk shifter was an enemy, Zachary would already be dead. He knew where he was staying. He knew where he was from. Vulnerability of Zachary's position was uncomfortable in his gut. He didn't have the upper hand sneaking into this place. Zachary would need the hawk's help to succeed.

Zachary didn't have patience. He needed to find some now.

Leaning his head back, he settled in to observe once again, but he heard the back elevator ding. He looked to the back of the room while the voice of the man in charge echoed over the speakers.

"Here come the girls, gentlemen. They'll provide you with tonight's fights and the statistics."

Heads of beautiful hair spread out and he braced himself for the scent of his mate.

CHAPTER 4

For a night like tonight, they would make rounds a couple times. This was the first, and there weren't many people here. Not the numbers they would have when the bell would ring and a fight began. Ezaray held her tablet in one hand against her chest and swayed around the room. Sickness twirled in her stomach from the eyes glancing at her healing marks on her face. There wasn't much left to heal. The doctor said another day or two and she'd look like herself again.

She wouldn't care about her appearance if her appearance wasn't one of the things keeping her alive. That and the sickening shine in the men's eyes at the sight of one of them hurt. She wondered if they thought of them like toys for a spoiled toddler. Magically fixed when broken and they never get taken away. The adrenaline in the room during a fight is disgusting. It's not a feel-good adrenaline. It's the kind of high that runs in a sociopathic child.

Ezaray and Holly walked next to each other until Holly tilted her head. She sighed through her angelic expression and veered off their path. Ezaray wanted to follow, but a man was waving her down.

"You're looking good, beautiful. When's your next fight?"

"Not until next season, I'm afraid." She ended her words with a sultry tilt to her head and brow.

"You're gonna win, right? I bet on you last time. I bet on you a lot." His voice darkened. If Tyrone allowed his clientele to threaten the girls, Ezaray was sure this man would have done just that now.

"I always do my best." Ezaray softened and moved back half a step.

"I heard that wasn't good enough." The man scoffed and turned his back on her. What did she care? Losing his money was his own damn fault. He didn't have to be down here gambling. But if it wasn't him, it would be someone else. The cycle would never end.

Ezaray continued her rounds, providing fighters and their stats for tonight's lineup and ignoring the leering eyes from each person she talked to. She went through the motions until she made it around the room. She spotted Holly talking to a man sitting down in shadows. Her features and posture were slipping. She would draw attention soon. Ezaray picked up her pace and made her way over. She set her hand on Holly's arm.

"You need to calm down." Ezaray whispered so as not to disturb the situation further.

"I'm fine." Holly's entire body changed, and she gracefully turned on her heel and walked away. Ezaray turned to see who she'd been talking to, intending to smooth things over with a club client. She froze at the sight of Zachary. His bright eyes stood out against his darker complexion and black hair. The snug, grey, button-up shirt outlined the shapes of his muscles. One ankle rested on the opposite knee and a glass with a finger of whiskey sat on his raised knee.

The air inside her body stilled with the dark power that came from him. But instead of a chill, warmth encased her. Her heart beat a little faster, urging her to move closer. She didn't have a connection with this man, but she felt one building. Ezaray feared what that would do to her.

"Hello, Ezaray." His rich, dark sound reached out and touched her, starting a flutter in her chest and it shivered down her body.

"Holly isn't happy you're here, is she?" She looked to Holly's retreating back then toward Zachary.

"No, she's not. Maybe you can talk to her." His disappointment rang through clear. "I'm not going away until I get the two of you out of here." He had the same kind of determination that Holly had when they were first brought here, but there was something more to him. A danger, a confidence, a strength. She wasn't sure. It was something neither herself nor Holly had. Then his words registered.

"The two of us? Why me? You don't know me. It's Holly you came for."

His free hand stroked his chin and tapped his pinched lips. "Are you allowed to sit with me?"

"Only if I'm giving you information."

"Information is exactly what I need." He raised his brow, the gesture looking more seductive than she believed he meant.

"Stats. I can give you stats."

"Then we'll start with that." He set his glass down on the table and grabbed the nearest chair from a neighbouring table and pulled it next to his. He waited for her to sit, returning to his position.

With trembling fingers, Ezaray swiped the tablet screen

to open it. "These are the girls fighting tonight." She pulled up the list. "And these are their overall wins and losses, and these are their most recent. And here are their KO's." She pointed to the columns of numbers beside the names.

She looked over at him, but his eyes were on her rather than the tablet. "How about you pretend to tell me all that information, but you answer my questions instead?"

Ezaray hesitated. If anyone walked by and heard what they were talking about, she'd be dead. And so would he.

"It's okay, Ezaray. I'll be watching." Even when coaxing and calm, he grumbled out what he had to say. But the smoothness reached her and calmed her senses. She felt protected, and she wished it could last.

"Okay," she said with a shaky whisper.

"Where do you all stay?"

"Upstairs." She pointed toward the top of the list on her tablet, a motion to follow her words. Her answers mumbled passed still lips and she looked as if she was sweet-talking him. "Offices turned into shared bedrooms."

"Who do you share with?"

"Holly, for now." She pointed to Holly's name on the list. "But that can change if handlers change."

"Handlers?" he asked sharply as if he already knew they weren't a good thing.

"There are eight handlers. They usually only manage two fighters at a time. We're traded between them often."

"They act like agents or team managers," he explained for her.

"Yes."

"Are you ever let outside the building?"

"No." That would be too easy. How many times had she wished to have even a moment of unconditioned air?

"What's in the back rooms?" He seemed to have enough

control over himself that when he asked about the back rooms, no part of him gestured toward them.

"A locker room without lockers and the doctor's offices."

"What's the doctor like?" Ezaray caught the suspicion in his slower question.

"Kind, I guess. His job is to keep us healthy. If we aren't healthy, we can't fight. If we can't fight, we don't make them money." She didn't need to say what came after that.

"Ezaray." She looked away from the screen at the sound of her name. "I'm going to get you out of here."

"Why me? Why only me and Holly?" She understood Holly's importance to him, but what importance did she have for him?

"If I can get everyone out and close this place down, I will. But my priority is you and Holly."

HER NEARNESS MADE BREATHING DIFFICULT. She calmed the beast within him, but he was weak with her scent overloading his senses. It wasn't the same debilitating state he'd been in the last time he'd been here. He felt more confident his strength would return with the more time he spent with her. Her sea-green eyes pinned him in place as he made a promise he was determined to keep.

"Don't give me hope." Her fake veneer plastered on her face didn't hide the fear escaping her lips. "Hope hurts. It hurts so much. We can't have it. We can't get out of here, and wishing and dreaming will just lead to painful disappointment. Please, don't give me that." She turned off the tablet and stood.

Her voice pierced his heart, sharp, jagged, and twisted. "Don't leave."

"I have to. I've stayed with you longer than I should have."

"One last question." She looked down at him with hurt, wide eyes. "Are the fights ever rigged?"

"Never. Something Tyrone prides himself on."

"Tyrone?"

"The man who owns it all. The one who announces everything from the ring."

He watched his mate walk away and sidle up to the next man she found. Jealousy hit him, but then he reached out to sense her emotions. So much sadness from a smile and cheery walk. She was trying to distract herself. She had to be. It's what he would do, what he was going to do. Distract from the helplessness. He couldn't let it invade and eat at his determination.

After all the information Ezaray had just given him, Zachary was eager to talk to the doctor later tonight.

He didn't wander while he waited for the fights to begin. The last thing he needed was to put his foot in his mouth by trying too hard. Zachary focused on his hearing, directing his attention to conversations nearby.

"Have you heard the rumours for this year's theme?"

"Not yet, but they should start soon. I'm not sure how he'll top last season's ending."

"Boxing princesses was a good one."

Zachary wanted to gag. He changed his focus to the next group.

"Who're you betting on tonight?"

"I'm not telling you. I'd rather win your money."

It was a game to them, treated no differently than gambling at a casino. The next conversation had rage bubbling and rising.

"I don't know where he finds his girls, but damn, he knows how to pick them. That's a fine ass."

"An ass that's gonna get beat tonight. No way she'll win. But it's a fight I'll enjoy watching."

Zachary closed off his hearing. Only for a moment. He drowned out the disgusting men, the clients of a place like this. A voice boomed over the sound system. He reluctantly pulled his attention back to his surroundings.

"Last chance to get information on your favourite fighter. The girls will disappear shortly, before returning later to take bets."

Zachary wanted to get up and chase after his mate, to find Holly.

Holly wanted him gone. She hadn't let him talk. Part of it felt like old times. The pint-sized, fiery sprite, telling him when he's wrong. Pointing a tiny finger at him when he tried not to laugh. But they weren't children now, and the fiery sprite he helped mold wasn't in her anymore. He could always see it behind her eyes. He'd thought it was odd to say that about someone, but it was there, something special and unique to her. Now, the best part of her was weak, beaten by her situation.

Holly had told him he needed to leave, give up, and go back to his life. She'd refused to tell him anything, answer any of his questions to help get them out. He was too late getting to her.

Zachary stood, surprised by his steady legs after having seen his mate, and went to the bar to get another drink. Again, he took the time to listen to conversations, to gauge the atmosphere. He forced his anger down. It wouldn't do any good. He moved around the room again, choosing a seat on the opposite side this time.

The next time the girls came out, eight were dressed for

fights and the other eight carried their tablets. They did the same as before, except instead of providing fighter information, they were taking bets.

Holly wore their fighters' uniform with wrapped hands.

Fuck. He hoped owl shifters had extra strength like the larger animals.

Holly caught his new position, most likely from his scent, and changed direction before she reached him. But Ezaray didn't.

Her scent infused his nose as she neared. Dizziness still spun in his head, but warmth also spread through him. He leaned forward and rested his elbows on his knees. As she walked past, he reached out and touched her wrist. She gasped and looked down at him.

The way her body relaxed gave him a thrill. Trust. She trusted him without knowing it.

He had words. He knew he wanted to speak, but nothing escaped. There was nothing he could say to her to make any of this better. He ran his thumb over the back of her hand and let her walk away.

HOLLY WAS the last fight of the night. Ezaray sat next to Maggie in the viewing box, trying not to cheer. It was difficult when Holly fought against Carmen. Holly had to pull back to make the fight last long enough, but no way would Carmen come out of this with a win.

Blood poured from a cut on the top of Carmen's forehead. Head wounds always bled more than they needed to. It ran down past the corner of her eye. Carmen growled loud enough they heard it from their viewing box. Holly's lip twitched, but then she readied herself for the onslaught that Carmen believed would give her the upper hand. And all it would really do is end the fight.

She charged forward, but her hand lowered an inch before she pulled back to strike. If Ezaray caught the move from here, then Holly wouldn't have missed it.

Holly stepped into Carmen's attack and her fist skated above Carmen's cocked one, landing a tough blow to her cheek. Carmen's head snapped to the side, and she stumbled. Her foot stomped out wide to catch her balance. She shook her head. Another step toward Holly and she had to thump another wide step. But she overcompensated and fell to the floor.

Gerard sidled up to Holly and raised her arm in the air, lifting her onto her toes. Tyrone announced the winner excitedly, but his eyes sparked with anger as he glanced down at Carmen. Ezaray knew that look. They all knew that look.

Carmen was in trouble.

As much as Ezaray hated the woman, she didn't wish the ending fate of this place on her. Who knew what kind of person she had been before she came here. It wasn't fair to judge someone based on how they acted when in captivity. She's scared, just like the rest of them. She's only trying to survive.

Carmen came to as Gerard escorted Holly to the back rooms. Soon Carmen was on her feet and following. The doctor close behind.

The fights were over and their jobs done. Security escorted them to the elevator to return to their rooms.

Ezaray allowed herself to search for Zachary in the crowd. She'd worked hard to keep her eyes away from him, but as she was about to leave the room, she wanted that connection. Something real.

Despite telling him not to give her any hope, he'd done it anyway.

His silver eyes cut across the room and latched onto her. She wanted to hold his gaze, reach for any form of warmth he could give her, but she didn't dare draw attention to either of them.

Her head throbbed and her muscles ached as she looked away and followed the rest of them to the elevator.

CHAPTER 5

Zachary's eyes heated. He held Ezaray's gaze as long as she allowed, but he had to close his eyes as soon as she looked away. When they heated, they were on their way to shifting to wolf eyes. Glowing, silver, wafers would stand out against his darker face if anyone looked his way. Once they cooled, he looked back toward Ezaray, but she was gone.

He'd stay at the club for a couple more hours. Only to observe the atmosphere after the fights, to study the security. And to watch the man that ran it all. He wanted to see where he went, where his focus was when the girls weren't there.

Tyrone sought the handlers of the winners, shaking hands and congratulating them. He made nice for about an hour, but as soon as he stopped talking to the men, a shadow fell over his face. An evil took its place as he walked straight passed Zachary and toward the elevator. The same elevator the girls left in.

Dread filled Zachary, but there was nothing he could do. Not if he still wanted a chance to get them out of here.

The muscles in his legs twitched, and he lifted his ankle to weigh them down. He waited for the hawk to appear. Finally, he did. Zachary stood and caught his attention before he disappeared at the bar.

"I figured you would have left."

"The head guy went upstairs with the girls. Is that normal?"

The shifter's jaw locked and his eyes flashed. "No. Unless a girl's in trouble."

"Who would be in trouble?"

"One of the losers. And I think I know which one. I just finished patching her up and sent her up to her room."

"Only she would be in trouble?"

"From what I know, yes."

"There's nothing you can do, is there?" Blinding rage started low in his core, but he kept it there. He wished he could destroy them all.

This time, when the doctor clenched his jaw, Zachary heard it pop out and back into place. His head shook once. "I need to leave." His voice was a strained, deep hum. He turned away from Zachary and stalked to the bar. The bartender set a whiskey in front of him and he poured it down his throat in one swallow.

Each step Zachary took toward the exit hurt. Worry caused a physical pain in his chest. His girl, his only sister and childhood friend he'd trusted, and his mate, stuck here.

He didn't have much time to get them out. Not before he lost his control and got them all killed.

Stepping outside, he breathed deep, pulling in the humidity into his lungs. Despite the rain over the previous days, it clung in the air with a promise that the storm hadn't yet arrived.

Zachary huffed. The air was a clone of his insides, a

storm brewing and ready to show its force. He walked the three blocks to the SUV and drove back to camp. He forced his mind onto Smoke rather than the women. It was the only way he made it there in one piece.

He hiked into the woods and sat on the ground, his back leaning against a tree. The rough bark poked through his too tight shirt. He smacked his head against the trunk and left it there to absorb the pain. Even with his eyes closed, he sensed Smoke coming near.

Moments later, Smoke rested the underside of his snout on Zachary's shoulder. He'd missed this. Even being reunited, they hadn't been as they used to be. They hadn't had the connection that made them strong. Zachary felt it rebuilding now, brick by brick. Paw by paw.

He lifted his hand and ran his fingers through the fur on Smoke's neck. And he felt the same content coming from the wolf. Never again would Zachary abandon him.

Not on purpose.

Zachary needed to tell him how dangerous this was. He needed to tell Smoke what to do if anything ever happened to him.

"Smoke," he started. The wolf tried to lift his head, but Zachary's hand firmed. "What I'm doing isn't safe. I will never abandon you again, but if something happens to me, I'd hate for you to go through what you did before."

Smoke nipped Zachary's chin, allowing the sharp teeth to pinch. His way of saying *Shut up.*

A screech sounded overhead, followed by an identical echo. One hawk landed in the tree above him and the other on the ground. Zachary watched the magic happen before the painful sounds of the shift began. Even as a hawk twice the normal size, the change looked to be more painful than it was for a larger animal like himself. More magic swirled in and out of the hawk to help the shift. It seemed not all shifters were the same. Asher would love to have a chat with the doctor hawk.

Naked, he sat against another tree, one knee bent and the other leg stretched out.

"I swear, I'm not one of them." Hatred spat from his mouth.

"Before you tell me who you really are, answer one question. Is there any way to get the girls out of there?" Zachary had decided to trust the hawk now that he'd sensed the animosity, the violence, toward Tyrone and the whole organization.

"Maybe. With a clear plan." The doctor shook his head.

"Okay. Start talking." Zachary leaned his head back.

"They forced me to be their doctor. They had my sister."

"Had?" Zachary didn't need to ask, but there was a hope his sister had escaped rather than the alternative.

"Maybe still has." His words were thick with pain. "Even without Tyrone holding my sister, I knew and saw too much. It was die or keep treating the girls. I couldn't leave the girls with who knew what kind of doctor they'd pick up next. I've stayed for them. I would have so much joy to watch that place burn. With all the men in it."

Zachary couldn't argue with the sentiment. He'd light the match.

"But I need to find out if my sister is still alive." He pulled in a deep breath. "You're turn. What are you doing there?" The doctor's agony dissipated and his eyes pierced Zachary.

"My cousin, basically my sister. She's one of them. I've been tracking her and trying to find her for over two years. And it turns out another one of the girls is my mate."

"Mate?" The doctor's head leaned forward.

"You hang around many other shifters?"

"No."

"Then I'll explain that one later." Now wasn't the time to dig into that. There was too much to explain when the focus needed to be on the girls.

"Which girls?"

"Holly and Ezaray."

"The owl shifter?" His lips twitched, and respect lit his expression.

"Yeah, I didn't know that until I saw her in there the first night. The last time I saw her was on her eighth birthday. She hadn't been a shifter then."

"They're two of the strongest fighters. Although, Holly has an advantage. Being a shifter, even a small animal, gives increased strength and abilities."

"What's your name?" He needed to act like Asher for the moment and learn more about the other shifter. Learn to trust him. Because there was no way Zachary could do this without him.

"Garrett Daly. Yours?"

"Austin Hall, but certain people call me Zachary."

"That's a stretch from Austin. Why?"

"It's my middle name. Holly has always called me Zachary. It's what the people I trust call me."

"Do you have a plan?"

"Get Holly and Ezaray out. Need to work out the rest." He had nothing but his goal. "Tell me everything about that place and I'll have a full plan. You want in on it?"

"Fuck, yes. But only if it doesn't put any of the girls in danger. And we get them all out." He was a true loyal protector. But protecting everyone made the job that much harder.

"I can't guarantee that. I came for Holly, and now Ezaray." He wasn't willing to make promises he couldn't keep.

"All or no help." Garrett threw down the ultimatum, pinning Zachary with cutting eyes.

"Fine. We'll try to get them all out." Zachary caved. As determined as he was, he wouldn't have the ability to leave anyone behind.

CARMEN PLEADED with screams and her terror, shrill and cold, slithered into every room. None of them could do anything to help her. A smack and a thump silenced her cries. The only sounds that followed were heavy footsteps and the ding of the elevator.

Ezaray covered her mouth to cover her own cries. They all mourned in silence for Carmen's fate. As it could be any of theirs some day. Guilt was always heavy on the winner of a fight that cost another their life. Holly's hollow eyes left room for a ghost that wasn't even born. Just as there was nothing any of them could do for Carmen, there was nothing they could do for Holly. This was life for all of them. It didn't matter how many times they told each other it wasn't their fault; it didn't help. And it never would.

The silence was devastating until an hour later when the hall flooded with footsteps. Each door opened one by one down the hall, followed by low tones. The door to their room blew open, but Gerard's beefy hand caught it before it hit the wall.

"In the lounge room." He stepped back until they left the room. The hall was full of the girls, their handlers, and security. They all crowded in the lounge. The security guards and the handlers circled the outer edge. Tyrone stood in the kitchen. His dark eyes met each pair of the girls' one by one.

As he met Ezaray's, she shivered as if he coated her in icy darkness.

Holly moved closer to Ezaray's side. They didn't wrap an arm around each other or hold hands. They gave the men nothing to hold against them. But knowing it was Holly's arm that touched hers in the crowded room stopped her shivers. Not the cold fear, but the visibility and her raw vulnerability rescinded.

"You'll notice there's one of you missing. Carmen's skills, and her actions, were unacceptable. Her fighting became sloppy, and she tried to compensate for that by offering her body to the handlers and myself. I've made it clear from the first day I brought each of you here, that no man in here will touch any of you that way. I will not put the financial security of this establishment at risk. If you can't fight, you can't bring in money. If you consistently lose, you can't bring in money. Fucking me, the handlers, or security will get you nowhere except a trip out of the building. Offering to fuck me, the handlers, or security will get you that same trip out of the building. Do I need to remind any of you of that destination or were Carmen's screams enough?"

No one answered him.

"Holly. Step forward." Holly pulled in a breath and stepped away from Ezaray toward Tyrone. The other girls parted to let her through. Holly stopped in front of Tyrone, but looked down to the floor. Tyrone tilted his head while staring at her in silence. He slowly pushed off the island and towered over her. Ezaray didn't see the motion past the other heads in the room, but he must have grabbed her chin because her head lifted, tilting further back than normal and at a side angle. "If I ever catch you pulling punches again, you will follow Carmen. Am I understood?"

"Understood." Holly's one word response whispered

across the crowd. A smug smile of a terrifying king stretched Tyrone's thin lips.

"Good." He released Holly and spun her around. He pushed her back to get her moving back to her place.

"Training tomorrow. For those that fought tonight as well, although you'll only observe for the morning. You're all dismissed. Security, please ensure the girls return to their rooms. Handlers, you all stay."

They left with security following in between the girls. No one spoke as the guards locked their doors behind each pair. Ezaray winced as the metal clicked into place. Tyrone rarely gave the order for security to lock them in their rooms. He must not want them to overhear what he was saying to the handlers.

Tyrone ruled this place. It was all his, and he made sure each person who walked in here knew that. The penalty of ruining what was his was severe.

Ezaray laid down on her bed and it surprised her when Holly lay down with her.

"You okay?" Ezaray whispered. She didn't want to disturb the quiet.

"You're all I have left to hold on to. If it's okay, I'll sleep beside you tonight."

"Always." Ezaray tilted her head sideways until it touched Holly's. They laid on their backs, neither ready to fall asleep. "Am I really all you have left to hold on to? Have you lost all hope?"

"A long time ago."

"What about Zachary?" Ezaray asked carefully, keeping her own hope and new attachment out of it.

"Zee, think about it. There's nothing he can do. He'll just get himself killed. And us with him."

"He was your hero. You've told me so many stories about him. Why wouldn't seeing him restore some of your hope?"

"Because the last thing I want is to watch him get killed, or any of us with him. If there was a way out of this place or if there was someone to come rescue us, we wouldn't be here."

"We can't stop him from coming back."

"I'm trying. Zee," she paused. "There's something about him you don't know."

"What is it?"

"I didn't even know until he showed up here. He's," Holly sighed. "It doesn't matter. We need to get some sleep. Training won't be easy tomorrow."

Ezaray wanted to push, but she didn't want Holly to move away. They needed each other and always would.

"WHAT I DON'T UNDERSTAND, is if you can get me inside so easily, how come you've never gone to the RCMP?" Zachary walked back from his tent with a pair of pants in his hand. He threw them at Garrett.

"I didn't say it was easy. As far as the RCMP, I couldn't chance any of them getting a get out of jail free card or Tyrone getting away with some of the girls. And if they ever caught the person inside, I'd have their death on my head. I do my best to keep every innocent person in there alive." Garrett clamped his jaw.

"But I'm okay to throw at them." Zachary's brow twitched as a drop of acidic bitterness bubbled. He was never good enough.

"No. You'd already made your way in the building, then refused to leave." The hawk had a point.

Zachary refused to abandon Holly, especially now that he finally found her. But he'd go to hell first before he'd abandon his mate. Garrett had tried to tell him to leave, but Zachary wouldn't listen.

"Then there's my sister. If I went to the police and it worked, I'd never find my sister with Tyrone behind bars. Or underground. I'm always looking for a way to save them, but I can't do it alone. And I'm not sure if we'll be able to do it alone either. Two men might not be enough."

"It will have to be. For now." If he called Asher and Nathan, they'd have help. "Have you ever found a way?"

"Tyrone is one meticulous bastard. Security is plentiful and tight. And those are the ones he trusts most. Security isn't just any hired thugs. They're well trained. I don't know what he has on them, maybe nothing, but they are his eyes and ears everywhere they go."

"Does he ever move the girls? Change locations?" There had to be a flaw in his organization.

"It's rare. He needs a reason."

"What kind of reason?"

"The possibility of getting caught. New attention. He has that building set up with businesses. If the lack of activity in the businesses becomes of interest, he'll move. He always has the next location and cover lined up."

"What's the process when he moves?"

"I've never been around when they do. He doesn't share information with those that don't need it. I'm only there to fix up the girls after their fights."

"Have any of the girls been around long enough to know?" It didn't sound like Tyrone gave up his girls easily, as long as they were winning him money.

"Yes. We can ask Holly and Ezaray."

"Has Holly ever said anything to you about being a

shifter?" It still shocked Zachary that Holly was an owl shifter. But more so the guilt of not being there for her, for not telling her about him when he had the chance. For not keeping in touch for more than a couple years over the phone after she moved.

"No. In fact, she never says a single word, but the look she gives me could kill if she had that ability."

"You're her kind. Not only another shifter, but a bird of prey. She feels betrayed."

"I've thought the same." Garrett closed his eyes.

"How often do you see the girls?"

"Only after the fights and for check-ups on those that fought. Unless another health emergency shows, but that doesn't happen and the girls don't confide in me."

"They think you're one of them."

Garrett nodded.

"What about the routines with security? Is the same guard always placed in the same spot?"

"No. And there are a lot of them."

"Fuck. This is near impossible." He understood more about why Holly was so sure they'd never escape.

"Near. But I don't think it is. There's another round of fights next week. We need time to find a way, but you can't be around long enough for them to think you're involved."

"And what about your involvement?"

"If we can't get them all out, then I have to stay behind. They can't know I'm involved." He was loyal to a fault.

"All right."

"Now, what were you saying about a mate?"

Zachary told Garrett how he met Asher and Gwen. Gwen's scent had confused him until he learned what she was. He filled Garrett in on everything they'd learned about the mates that Fate chose for them. Sticking to the assumption that all shifters would have one. "Your mate's scent will be stronger than any other. You'll experience dizziness, nausea, and pain until you acclimate to what her scent does to your system."

"Sounds interesting," he said with skepticism.

"So far, it doesn't seem we have a choice." Although Zachary hadn't tried to fight it. Fighting it would leave Ezaray in a fate worse than what she was already in.

"At least, now I know." Garrett nodded. "How did you find Holly?"

Zachary hesitated, but it really didn't matter. "Have you ever seen a ghost?"

Garrett huffed. "All the time."

"Long hair and dress." The woman looked identical whenever she appeared, both at the end of Asher's wedding and again at Nathan's when she told him where to find Holly.

"Transparent. Pale eyes. A rope necklace." Garrett finished his description. "Yeah, I've seen her." He spoke with more familiarity than Zachary felt.

"She told me," he finished.

"I'm thinking I should have introduced myself to your crew a while ago."

"I'm thinking the same. How much do you know about her?" Zachary would love to know what Garrett knew about the woman.

"I know some. She is a ghost."

"Was she a witch?" He, Asher, and Nathan had their suspicions, but couldn't confirm it.

"Yes. She's helped me keep the girls safe."

"How?" Zachary frowned.

"I use her recipes for medicines and ointments for them. None of them have scarred or developed serious illnesses, at least that I know of. She doesn't tell me anything about herself, and I see her less often now that I've learned all I needed from her." She didn't seem to show up unless she had something to tell them.

"Does your wind get excited to see her?" The two times Zachary had seen the woman, the winds hovered close to her as if seeing a lost loved one. He believed that was the case.

"Yes. I've asked her about that, but all she does is smile."

Zachary sighed. Maybe someday they would learn who she was, and hopefully learn where shifters came from.

CHAPTER 6

B rutal best described their training that morning. They watched for every flinch, falter, misstep, and forcefully corrected each one with harsh words that seared. No praise given for a good job, but they all knew when they did something right from the gleeful expression on their handler's face. Tyrone glowered through the entire training session, but he glowered at all the best fighters. A chilling worry settled inside Ezaray. To be under that man's focus was disturbing.

He caught Holly pulling back the night before. Being a shifter, there was a delicate balance. She'd done well until now to hide it most of the time. Never did it seem like she was stronger than her opponent, only better.

But last night, Tyrone saw something Holly hadn't intended him to see.

Even having fought the night before, they only allowed Holly to rest for the morning. After the noon break, she trained alongside Ezaray, just as hard as the rest of them.

They let them break enough for water when needed and a single snack in the afternoon. They made them lift weights, use the punching bags, and several sparring matches with each other. Ezaray didn't understand their purpose of such a gruelling day. It did nothing except exhaust them all, even Holly. Since the fight the night before and on such little sleep, she didn't have to act out her fatigue.

Ezaray huffed. It donned on her. Tyrone and the handlers watched for stamina. Especially in the best fighters. To know when they waned in strength and when they pulled punches in a fight. This wasn't a normal training day, and they had a reason.

Ezaray didn't know the time when they finally allowed them to leave. They all took turns showering, not enough strength for speech between them, then wandered into the lounge to eat. Tonight, no one complained when Holly, Ezaray, and a couple others worked together to cook for everyone. The girls that had followed Carmen stayed quiet. With Carmen's death, they've realized there isn't a safe position to be in. Ezaray felt for them, but it was best they learned this lesson before it was too late, before they ended in the same place as Carmen. And since their behaviour had followed hers, that was where they would go.

Even though she hated Carmen, Ezaray wished it didn't take a lesson like that for one of them to realize.

The only sounds in the room were people's movement and the sound of silverware on dishes, the clink echoing through the lounge. The girls usually chatted with one another. But with a loss sind the day of training, no one had the energy, or the spirit.

Tyrone didn't kill girls unless he had to. So there would be times they'd go through long stretches without losing anyone. It sometimes created a false sense of security. But that didn't douse the fear-fueled anger at the man that controlled their lives and their right to live. Especially after losing two girls this month. Kate, right before Zachary had shown up, and now Carmen.

Ezaray never felt safe. Their lives and their statuses were unstable. She wouldn't let herself forget, couldn't afford to forget if she ever had any hope of escaping.

She could tell herself her hope no longer existed, and maybe it didn't. Being as connected to Holly as she was, her emotions had always mirrored hers. But seeing someone they could trust from outside the building, exposed what little hope still lingered, too stubborn to leave her. His silver eyes and the heat from his skin touched her inside and stayed with her.

Ezaray lay down in bed after helping clean some dishes, leaving the rest for the last of the girls to wander in. Holly did the same. Ezaray wanted to talk to her. She wanted to know more about Zachary. Holly had been about to tell her something about him, but cut herself off. Ezaray found herself more curious about Holly's childhood friend than she'd ever been. Now that she'd seen him for herself, felt his touch, she wanted to hear the stories of them growing up all over again.

"Holly?" Ezaray turned her head to look across the room at her. Holly slowly shook her head.

"I can't talk tonight, Zee." Holly's bruised voice worried Ezaray. It wasn't her own. It was like looking at the beginning of the end of her best friend.

ZACHARY HAD MEMORIZED the blueprints of the building after making the adjustments that Garrett told him. Since being in that building, they'd changed the exits and entrances. Many had been closed off and unused to restrict access from patrons and to ensure the girls stayed where Tyrone wanted them.

Stepping into the club area, his eyes roamed to connect the blueprints to the reality. What neither he nor Garrett knew for sure were if the blocked off elevators worked. A security guard's passkey could gain access to all stairways, but they rarely used them, even by the guards themselves. At least as far as Garrett understood. He didn't frequent between fights, unless treating the girls.

After going in yesterday morning to check on Holly and the other girls who'd fought the night before, Garrett had discovered the entire group in an intense training session. And the girl who'd fought against Holly wasn't there.

He'd come back to the campsite in a foul mood, and after he described what he saw, Zachary felt the same. Danger hung over the girls in a thick cloud waiting to strike at each of them, and as much as he only cared to get Holly and Ezaray out, he couldn't leave the rest of them in that uncertain hell.

They'd decided that whatever plan they made had to involve all the girls. He didn't lie to himself, though. If it came down to a decision, he would choose Holly and Ezaray first.

The hawk ambled, doing his usual rounds, acting the part as a member of the organization, before checking on the girls. Zachary wore the same blue shirt he'd worn the first night and sat at the bar longer than the previous nights. He needed a better vantage point to see over the tops of heads. His chair in the alcove created a hidden spot with no view. Great for blending in, not so great for observing every-thing, so he stayed at the bar.

Two hours passed before any of the guards moved, but

they never left the space empty. New ones replaced half the number of guards on the floor, and that half moved to new stations to relieve the rest. Zachary bet this structure ran as a well-oiled machine. He wondered how complacent the guards were and if they all recognized each other well. Almost any plan from the inside would have to involve the guards.

Garrett planned to talk to Holly during her checkup before tonight's fights, and Zachary would do the same if he saw either her or Ezaray. Zachary warned Garret that talking to Holly wouldn't be easy. She'd already shut Zachary out within two minutes of seeing him. Just as feisty as always, but her focus had been turned. She looked down a despairing path and refused to turn back around.

Zachary couldn't guarantee their escape, but he could guarantee he wouldn't give up.

Tyrone sounded overhead. "There are two fights tonight, gentlemen. My girls will be around soon. Enjoy your evening." A measure of his enthusiasm was lacking from his lower tone. It set Zachary's nerves on edge. It could be nothing. It could be the loss of the girl. Zachary hoped that was all it was. He didn't want surprises.

Garrett sat down beside him at the bar, but didn't look at him. He spoke low with barely a movement from his lips. The volume was enough that as a shifter, they could hear each other fine.

"You were right. Holly refused to tell me anything, although she spoke to me for the first time."

"What did she say?"

"Fuck you, you disgusting sky rat."

Zachary kept himself from spitting out his drink, and if he hadn't had a drink in his mouth, he would have outright laughed. That was his Holly. Hell, he'd taught her all the curse words when she was way too young to know them. Not always intentionally.

"That's funny to you?" Garrett lifted the glass the bartender set in front of him.

"It's comforting. A piece of her is still in there." But Zachary worried how long that would last. And he needed to know the state of his mate. "Was Ezaray in there too?"

"She was, but Holly forbade her from speaking."

Zachary drained his glass. They needed information from the girls to help get them out. If the two they knew and trusted wouldn't talk, they'd be working blind. They didn't want to involve the other girls until the last minute, maybe not even then. Their plan and Garrett's involvement had to be confidential. If any of the girls turned loyal to Tyrone, taking their chance with him rather than risk their life with an escape, they'd fail. They wouldn't take that risk. Not with only one shot at this. Tyrone was too careful.

Zachary stood, saying nothing else to Garrett. He ambled to the back of the room, finding a similar seat to the side to settle in. This one gave him a better view of the back rooms and doors. He'd move when the girls made their rounds, but for now he wanted to see what happened with security when they entered. He wanted to gauge the attitudes of the guards.

The elevator dinged. Ezaray was the first out. Her dark hair had a low glow under the yellow lights. Sweet relief struck his heart when he saw her hands free of wraps.

She didn't see him when she started walking the room, but her steps halted for half a beat and her head turned to the side. As she kept moving, she turned her head fully and caught his eye. Her lips parted. She'd sensed him. He hated that he knew how important she was to him and she had no idea, thinking she was only a friend of the one he was really looking for.

He needed to touch his mate.

Zachary hated himself for breaking her eye contact, but he had a job to do. He inhaled her scent, hoping it gave him strength instead of weakness. Looking back toward the guards, he watched their eyes, their hands, their mouths. Any twitch might tell him something about their feelings, their moods, toward their job or the girls.

One guy eyed the ass of the redhead Ezaray fought his first night here, his lips lifting on one side before straightening quickly and veering his attention away. Another made a fist and hid it by his other hand in the front. He despised something about this. It wasn't enough for Zachary to come to any conclusions. Other than those movements, the guards were unreadable.

He eyed their stations at the door. They stood in front of the blocked off elevator and the back rooms. There was no space to move past them. The elevator the girls came through though had space with the guard standing to the side of it. A thin plaque with the words "Fighters Only" hung above the doors.

Zachary stood to follow the girls' trail and put himself in a position to stop Ezaray or Holly. He hoped to talk with both of them, but figured Holly would avoid him.

He spotted Holly first and ducked to the side. She might still catch his scent, but he hoped it would be too late.

And it was. She stepped directly beside him and veered further out when he spoke. She was far enough away he needed to put on an act.

"Excuse me." He heard her teeth grind together as she turned. She stepped close, so she didn't have to speak over the crowd.

"Why are you still trying? And why does the doctor want to ask me questions?" An accusatory growl reverberated from her throat and escaped through the fake expression she held frozen on her face.

"I told you I'm not giving up. Holly, I've been searching since the day you disappeared." The pain he'd felt for those two years still surprised him, was still there.

"This is my life, Zachary. You can't save me from this." She said it with extreme confidence.

"I can't if you don't help us." He tried not to beg.

"Us? How can you trust him?" One eye twitched with mistrust.

"He's not the bad guy, Holly. Please. There's more you don't know, but I need to get you out of here to show you, to tell you. I've found more shifters. We're building a life. One you deserve to be part of."

"Don't do this to me." Her shields and act slipped.

"Think about it, Squirt. But don't think long. We'll be acting as soon as possible. We're getting you out whether you like it or not. Or die trying."

"That's what I'm afraid of." She took one step backward, then a second, before turning on her heel. Her head was down while she regained her composure, then as she lifted her head, he saw her act back in place from her profile. If he had found her any later, then it might have been too late to save her from herself.

THE HEAT that ran through her veins from Zachary's stare stunned Ezaray. It hurt when he turned away from her, which was ridiculous. They had to look away. That kind of stare would be noticeable to the wrong people. But he was an anchor to her now. Just the thought of him ignited the flame inside her. And the sight of him gave her warmth. She hadn't known her own warmth had been missing until now. She didn't want to let him or the chance of escape go.

The doctor had visited Holly before they came down. He said he wanted to ask some questions. Wanted to help rescue them all. Holly refused to help and when Ezaray spoke up, Holly pinned her with her glowing owl eyes. "Don't say a damn word, Zee. He isn't who he says he is."

Holly gave her the same cryptic message she did about Zachary. There was something more to both men. Something that made Holly despise the doctor and be wary of her hero.

Ezaray hated going against her best friend, but if it benefited both of them and all the girls in there, she would. Holly would forgive her after.

She'd talk. She'd tell the doctor what he wanted to know. And she'd tell Zachary.

It took considerable effort not to search for him as she did her duties with the men around the room. She rushed through each conversation as much as she could without being impolite. Need burned inside her to see him, to feel his small touches.

She'd laid awake for hours trying to push this blossoming connection to Zachary away, far away. She wanted out and to help him, but had to hold on to some reality in case it didn't work. In case this really was her life. Then she had to wonder if she would ever give up or continue to survive.

Ezaray didn't know. She'd buried the person she used to be, and she wasn't even sure if it was within herself anymore. Maybe a part of her soul escaped and lived the life it should elsewhere, in a land that kept it happy.

At the end of the room, she saw Holly. Her eyes glossed above her smile. Zachary must have spoken to her. It was the only thing that could get to her like that anymore. Ezaray took a deep breath and pulled in patience. She'd find him on her way around.

And there he was, just on the other side of the ring. He didn't hide from her, and she let her eyes find his.

Zachary held out a chair, inviting her to sit. She did, but kept some distance. He held his hand out and she set hers in his, landing with the weight of a feather, bracing herself for the heat that came with his touch.

So large, his fingers wrapped around hers, hiding them from sight. He sealed in the heat. Her attempt to keep the touch light to protect herself didn't work.

"Are you all right?" The sound of his voice, rich and soothing, added to the heat of his hand.

"I am."

"I have some questions I need you to answer." He pretended an interest in her tablet.

"Okay."

"Have you been here when locations have changed?"

"Yes, but it was only a few days after we arrived. I'm not sure how much I can tell you."

"Do your best."

"We're moved in pairs at different times. I don't know if it's the same vehicles used over and over or if they take each pair in separate ones. That day was terrifying." It all blurred in her mind, but she remembered how disgusting she'd thought the handlers were and how lethal the security guards appeared as they were ushered from one place to the next. Tyrone had always been at the next destination. His presence seemed to follow them like some demonic shadow.

"Thank you. That helps. Can you think of anything else?"

"I think it's the handlers that drive their own girls, but I can't be sure. I don't remember the faces from the first few months."

"Are there any girls that have been here longer than you and Holly?"

"Maggie. The girl I fought the first night you were here. But she doesn't speak." She looked down at her tablet. "I should move."

His hand squeezed hers before he released her and leaned back with an expression that matched most men in the room. His entire appearance blended in with the top bidders, except for his eyes when he looked at her. Silver heat.

"Stay safe."

Ezaray stood and on shaky legs walked away from the one thing she discovered she needed most. She'd thought it was Holly, that it would be Holly that would pull her through. But it was this man that had the strength she longed for.

CHAPTER 7

During a move was a possibility, but he needed more information. From the girl that didn't talk.

Zachary didn't know what emotion would win within him, frustration or excitement. This operation had been looking impenetrable until now. But even with this opportunity, too many complications still stood in the way.

He watched his mate walk away from him once again. He craved to touch her, to hold her, to breathe her in. Sweet cherries hovered in the air in front of him. It wasn't enough.

Zachary had one more question that only Holly could answer. He stalked her around the ring and stopped in front of her. Her focus had been off and he caught her off guard.

"Does Ezaray know what you are?" He looked down at her with an interest that made him sick, but he needed to put on an act as much as the girls if he spent too much time here.

"Yes. I told her years ago."

"Holly, I should have told you about me. I started to, so many times."

"It's okay, Zachary." Sweet sympathy rang through her

words. For only this moment, her bitter anger wasn't at the surface. "I wouldn't have told a friend eight years younger either. And Ezaray is the only one I've ever told. I wanted to tell you though."

Guilt, sharp and jagged, made breathing hard. He never should have stopped calling her. He should have gone to see her.

"Have you told her about me?" He craved for Ezaray to know, but not in a place like this.

"No. Not yet."

Zachary side-stepped, ready to move away, but paused. "Don't lose all your hope yet, Holly. Please." He walked away before he saw her reaction. His Holly was still in there, but fading away and it scared him.

He grabbed another drink from the bar and found a secluded seat on the other side of the room to settle in. He stayed until the end of the fights, admiring the skills of the girls. Every single one that was still alive in all this was amazing. This wasn't a part of any of them, but they all possessed so much strength to learn the way they have to survive. He hoped when they were free, they recognized that strength and continue to live their lives knowing they're special.

Fuck. This place wasn't good for him. He needed to mind his thoughts if he intended to blend in. Thoughts like those could give him away.

Garrett left the elevator after taking the fighters back to their rooms. Their eyes connected for a moment as he passed and left the club. Zachary waited to give him time to get away from the building before he started his exit. He reached to set his empty glass on the bar, but his shifter hearing piqued at the mention of Tyrone from a nearby security guard. He followed through with the motion and sat down, nodding for the refill the bartender offered.

"Tyrone ordered another girl. The Mountain Shipping Line has replaced Damien and is back to running as normal. It will be at least a week for shipment."

"I don't mind the girls once they've been broken in, but the new ones get on my nerves."

"Do you expect them to walk in with smiles on their faces?"

"No, but it'd be nice."

Zachary downed his drink and left the empty glass on the bar. Urgency coursed through his blood. This gave them a deadline. And he wanted to ask the hawk if he knew about another girl.

He reached the camp and sniffed the air. Smoke wasn't far into the tree line and a hawk sat high above him, but it was the doctor's pair. Garrett stepped out of the trees and sat on a log placed by the fire. Zachary followed him.

"Do they tell you when they're bringing in new girls?"

"Not until they arrive. And I only see them if they were hurt on the way." His eyes moved with the flames the higher they rose.

"They're bringing a new one. I overheard a couple guards as I was about to leave. Tyrone ordered another girl from the Mountain Shipping Line, but they aren't expecting her for at least a week."

"I thought the shipping line was in shambles." Garrett turned a frown on him, and Zachary wondered how much of that he knew. He said he'd been watching him, Asher, and Nathan, but how closely. Zachary wouldn't believe he got close enough to find out their personal information without at least one of them sensing the hawk. Did Garrett know how Zachary had worked his way into the shipping line to get close to Damien Marks, to find where he shipped girls?

"I assumed it was too, but I guess they've replaced Damien and are back to work."

"The Mountain Shipping Line isn't Tyrone's only source for girls, so it doesn't matter, anyway." It had only been a matter of time before the next evil stood up.

"Ezaray said Maggie has been there longer than her and Holly."

"Yeah, she's right. The problem with Maggie is she doesn't talk. At all. I worry about her."

"Ezaray also said they moved locations after they arrived, but she doesn't remember much. Holly might remember more and so should Maggie." Those three girls were going to be their best source of information, but without enough access to them, it limited that information.

"If we can give him a reason to move, we could get the girls out then." The doctor sounded hopeful.

"They take the girls out of the building in pairs."

"That's helpful." His eyes thinned, no doubt thinking the same thoughts Zachary had. Minimal guards and only two girls at a time.

"What's his process for a fire? Or damage to the building?" Now, they needed a reason for Tyrone to move locations.

"That would depend on the severity and how much attention it would draw. I don't know, but that's something I should be able to find out. I'm not even informed of those details. He doesn't trust me as it appears he does."

"Security is tight and strict with schedules. They're also visible wherever they are." Zachary spent a lot of time observing the guards. "Getting through them to get them out might not be possible." It posed too much risk of getting caught.

"Not for all the girls."

"So forcing him to move is our best option."

"Do we wait for the new girl?" Hesitancy slowed Garrett's question.

"I don't know. I don't think we can pass if the opportunity shows itself, but she may also already be here by the time we can act."

"You're right." They both imagined what the girl's fate would be if they captured her, but never handed over to Tyrone's organization. She'd be sold off to the highest bidder. Garrett looked as if he was already shouldering that burden. "We'll need help."

And that was what Zachary didn't want to need.

◢

Despite the late hour and that they should both be asleep, Ezaray could hear Holly's quieter and uneven breathing.

"I talked to Zachary." Her voice faded as she spoke, the initial sound too loud in the night.

"What did you say?" Ezaray expected Holly to be mad. She didn't expect the curiosity she heard.

"He asked if we've ever moved locations. I told him I couldn't remember much." She'd been running through that night in her mind since she'd talked to him. But it may as well have been a lifetime ago, and she had been a different person.

"I remember some of it, but I didn't understand enough about this place then."

"You're not mad at me?"

"No. It's all hopeless, but I don't have control over him.

He's going to do this, no matter what I tell him." Holly rolled over onto her side and the light of the city shone on her face. She looked so tired. Ezaray wondered if she didn't have the strength she did, if Holly wouldn't fade away and give up like others have.

"Will you help?"

"Yeah, I think so." She sighed. "Zee, I'm sorry."

"For what?"

"For letting go," she whispered, sounding as sad as teardrops looked. Holly confirmed Ezaray's fear.

Ezaray locked her jaw.

No. This couldn't be the life meant for them. And now Zachary had shown up. There was her hope. But she had to ask herself if she was willing to take on the risk of death by attempting to escape with him. Not only her death, but all of them.

"What were you going to tell me about Zachary the other night?"

Holly's eyes darted away. Ezaray sat up in bed and crossed her legs.

"Holly, please. You've let go, but I haven't and I don't want to. What do I need to know about him?"

"He's a shifter. A wolf." Holly slowly moved herself into the same position and met Ezaray's eyes.

"A shifter like you?" Holly said she'd never found others. That was why she told Ezaray her secret at fifteen. Holly had been so alone and needed someone to share that part of her. "When did you find out?"

"When he first arrived. I smelled him. He never told me, then I moved away the day before I became an owl." Holly took in a shaky breath and sighed. "I don't know if him being a wolf will help us get out. Being a shifter in here hasn't helped."

"He believes he can."

"Oh, and the doctor is a shifter too."

"What?" For the two years they'd been here, Holly had kept that to herself. It explained her attitude toward him.

Ezaray remembered the first thing she ever said to him the other night. *Fuck you, you disgusting sky rat.*

Ezaray's laughter wouldn't stay in. It was the first time she'd laughed in over two years. The bubbling feeling twirled in her stomach and up her esophagus like an upside down tornado.

"What is it?" Holly's eyes widened with worry.

"You called him a sky rat. What animal is he?"

"A hawk." The sight of Holly's lips twitching upward, a genuine lift in her mood followed by a single chuckle, it shocked Ezaray. She'd missed her friend despite being by each other's side through all of this. They weren't themselves, and suddenly Ezaray had a deep need to return to a life that was worth living. For all of them.

IT WAS difficult to change his focus, but Zachary needed Smoke to know he was still with him. Once the late season campers had settled for the night, he hiked into the woods and met up with Smoke. He stripped and shifted.

The warmth of the grey wind tingled through his veins until an ache throbbed deep in his muscles. Taking slow breaths, he embraced every bit of the magic until he landed on four paws on the ground. His appreciation for it grew deeper. When he'd returned from his initial search for Holly, he'd shifted and searched for Smoke for so long. When he couldn't find him, Zachary stayed human, resisting the animalistic needs inside him.

Now, shifting next to his only brother added strength to the magic within him, the magic that controlled him.

Up for a run? He asked Smoke.

Always.

Zachary needed the time to think. It wasn't only the upcoming escape plan, but he wanted a moment to consider what came after that. Maybe that was stupid, but it'd been rare there were times he was happy with his life. He had a chance now. It wouldn't be easy to help the girls cope after this, but he will do whatever it takes.

He'd never understood people's mistrust of him growing up, not until he was older and learned that who he thought was his father wasn't. His biological father had been a deadbeat who couldn't hold a job simply due to a bad attitude. He'd abandoned Zachary and his mother only a few months after Zachary had been born. It hadn't taken long for his biological father's best friend to step up in his place. Zachary had grown up with loving parents and a home.

But the trail of the deadbeat followed him around Hull Creek. It was a shit excuse, but he couldn't control opinions. Zachary had been the kid that other parents didn't want their children playing with. They gave him a side eye when they passed at the schoolyard during pick ups and drop offs. Those looks said, "We're watching you and waiting for when you'll screw up. Just like your old man."

Not long after he'd first shifted, he'd overheard a mother ask her son, "Does that kid get in a lot of fights?" The kid shrugged. He'd overheard many questions like that with his new shifter hearing. Without Holly around after she moved, Zachary had been a little lost and embraced whatever misconceptions people had. He didn't have to watch what he did when he didn't have someone looking up to him.

It was the same with the wolves. He hadn't been accepted because he wasn't a true wolf.

He'd started following the kids that got into trouble. The most trouble Zachary had gotten in were fights, not that anyone would believe him.

But now, he'd found acceptance. Asher and Gwen. They'd taken Smoke in when he needed family most. Kai, Asher's pair, welcomed him as part of the pack. And they'd all taken Zachary in too.

He had a new family, one he and Smoke got to choose and who chose them in return.

A family that Zachary didn't want to put in danger, but the help might be necessary and he trusted no one else.

Smoke and Zachary ran side by side, weaving around trees and moving farther and farther from the city. His ears twitched with sounds of animals, small and large. Smoke caught his gaze and another broken piece fixed itself inside him.

There was still so much they both needed to be whole again. For Smoke, that was going back to settle in Alder Ridge with Kai's pack permanently. For Zachary, that was getting Holly and Ezaray out and then settling in Alder Ridge. The plan to move there with Smoke had been floating in his mind for a long time. But now, it was something Zachary wanted too. Settling in with his mate.

Twin hawks screeched overhead, and the wolves slowed their run to see where the hawks would land. They swooped down to a boulder a few metres ahead. Zachary and Smoke trotted up to them.

I've got some answers for us. Garrett shook his feathers and resettled his wings. *Their process of getting out of the building is the same, no matter what the reason. Of course, if it's a fire or building damage, they'll move them out faster. The build-*

ing's alarm system has been disabled and replaced with basic detectors. No authorities will be notified by the alarm.

Gives them time to clean up their shit before anyone comes in. Did you find out what their entire process is? That was the most important piece of information left.

Only what we already know. Claws stretched and scraped against the stone. Zachary winced at the sound. Not as bad as nails on a chalkboard, but with his sensitive hearing, it was close.

There's nothing more we can do until we find that out. We need to hope Holly remembers, or we need to talk to Maggie. The run had left Zachary calm, and he didn't mind letting go of this for another hour. *I'd say run with us, but that would be a hilarious sight. Come fly.*

Zachary didn't wait for an answer. He took off at a run and gave Smoke a wolfish smile as he caught up and turned the run into a race. Garret must have hesitated because it took longer than expected for them to hear the screech of the two hawks. With a quick glance up, he saw the two birds flying in loops around each other and through the trees.

As he let go for the time they had left, Zachary thought of home. What home used to be for him, what it was with Asher, Gwen, Nathan, and Shaye. And he thought of what it would be when he took Ezaray and Holly back to Alder Ridge.

CHAPTER 8

Ezaray now looked for a chance to talk to Maggie. The doctor had been in to check on Holly one last time, but as she'd already healed faster than normal, he didn't need to. It was for show. He kept to the same appointment schedule for her as he did the rest. He'd tried again with Holly.

"Will you answer some questions?"

"I'm thinking about it." Her slow response still gripped her mistrust, and Ezaray expected the same sky rat insult to escape.

"I'm not thinking about it anymore." Ezaray hoped her friend wouldn't stop her this time as she continued to speak up. "But I've already said everything I remember."

"Can you girls talk to Maggie?" The doctor looked between the two of them. The colour of his eyes had the same odd swirl Holly's did. Ezaray didn't know how she never noticed that before.

"I'll try." She didn't need to explain to the doctor that Maggie didn't speak. He looked again at Holly and held her gaze. She narrowed her eyes and nodded once.

So here they were, looking for Maggie in the lounge. She never stayed in here long.

There, sitting closest to the kitchen, but she'd almost emptied her plate. They didn't want any of this to look suspicious.

Holly went to the kitchen and Ezaray sat with Maggie. It wasn't anything they'd done differently before.

"Maggie," Ezaray muttered her name. She looked up. "We need your help with something."

Maggie looked back toward the kitchen where Holly was making a salad, then caught Ezaray's gaze.

"Is there a reason you don't talk?" Ezaray gentled the question, ensuring she held no judgment. Maggie lifted one shoulder, but not high. The gesture was more protective than it was an answer. "You've been here longer than us and we need your help to remember."

Holly set a couple plates on the table and sat down across from Maggie. "Please."

Maggie nodded, but her head didn't make the full movement. It barely bobbed before she took her plate to the kitchen and left the lounge.

"Was that a yes?" Holly looked over at Ezaray.

"I think so."

Later at dinner, Holly and Ezaray were already settled when Maggie came. She avoided them. Ezaray didn't want to ask her again, not so soon. Putting pressure on her wouldn't get them what they needed. Even considering helping an escape was risky. Ezaray was willing, but that didn't mean terror didn't fill her core.

"We can't force her." Holly looked down at her plate.

"I know. She might just need time." Or she was sneaky in her own right.

Ezaray startled when their bedroom door opened a few

hours later, but Holly only stood. Maggie walked through, a couple books in her hand. She passed each of them a book, then sat down at the very end of Ezaray's bed. She swallowed and winced as she opened her mouth.

"Those are just a cover for coming in here." Her words rasped, but her sound rolled sweet and husky. "But you're welcome to read them anyway."

"How did you get books?" Holly's fingers gently stroked the cover.

"The last building we were in had lots of books. I stole as many as I could before we moved."

"Moving is what we wanted to ask you about." Ezaray hugged the book to her chest, but stayed on task while Maggie spoke. "How do they do it? We only remember a little. We hadn't been here long before the last move."

"You can't escape. You may be out in the air, enjoy that while you can, but there's no escape for us."

"Can you still tell us how they get us out?" Holly leaned forward. Ezaray could see her comfort, and she recognized the two had similar attitudes toward escaping.

"They take us in pairs. Your handler and one security guard take you from the building and to a waiting car. Once that car has left, they take the next pair down, but not immediately after."

"Where's Tyrone during it?" Holly had the more critical mind.

"Already at the new location." Maggie scooted further back on the bed rather than perched on the edge.

"Do they check in with him during transportation?"

"I don't remember them making any calls, but that doesn't mean they didn't."

"How long have you been here, Maggie?" Ezaray tilted her head and tried to catch Maggie's gaze.

"I don't know anymore." She pulled her knees up and wrapped her arms around them. "Why do you guys want to know all this?"

Ezaray looked at Holly, unsure how much to say.

"Why do you think?" Holly didn't snap the question back at her, but she turned it around to allow for Maggie to fill in the blanks. It was for the best. No one else needed to know about Zachary and the doctor. And none of the other girls needed to know about the escape plan. "Can you promise not to tell anyone?"

"I don't speak, remember." Maggie's lips twitched.

"Why don't you speak?" Ezaray permitted her curiosity to ask.

"I spoke too much when I first got here. I won't say or do the wrong thing again." She stretched her legs and stood. "I've been in here too long. Goodnight." Maggie left as quietly and gently as she came in.

"How do you think Zachary and the doctor will do it?" Ezaray stroked the book absentmindedly. A piece of normal, and even if Maggie hadn't said a single word, she'd given them a gift.

"I don't know, but once we tell them, it's up to them." Her eyes flashed and there ended Holly's involvement.

PAIN SLICED as Zachary showed interest in the other fighters and not Ezaray. She'd told him what Maggie remembered, and Holly filled him in on her memories of the last move. He wanted to keep his space until he could get them out. And it hurt. The physical ache grew with every other girl he looked at. Zachary wanted to leave, but he stayed until the end of the fights and until the doctor had disappeared in the back with the fighters.

Back in the woods, he paced, kicking sticks and rocks out of his way while he waited for the hawk to show up. Smoke twitched and adjusted on the ground under a tree. Zachary's agitation affected him. He fought the urge to shift and run with Smoke, give the animal freedom, but he needed to talk to Garrett.

Smoke lifted his head and Zachary followed the same sound. A car parked at his campsite. Light steps sounded through the darkness. Zachary's eyes flashed and adjusted to the dimness to see the tall frame of Garrett walking toward him.

"You're agitated. Did the girls tell you anything?"

"Yeah. Ezaray was right." Zachary stopped moving once Garrett caught up to him. "They move them in pairs with one handler and one security guard. There's time between each pair that goes. They're unsure if there's contact from each car on the way."

"And Tyrone?" So much hatred in the sound of his name.

"Already at the new location."

"But that wouldn't be the case during an emergency." Garrett had frowned and shook his head, thinking through the same logistics as Zachary.

"No. My guess is he'll either be the first out or the last out." It's what he would do if he were running the organization.

"Probably dependent on the attention the emergency is getting."

"We can do this." Zachary tried not to sound eager, but determination leached through his words.

"For all the girls." Garrett suffered from a guilty conscience. And he was the type of man to never leave someone behind. A doctor that cared too much for his patients.

"The only way we can get all the girls is if they don't find out the girls are being rescued until we have them all."

"We need more people."

Zachary hesitated. Garret wasn't wrong, but he didn't want to bring Asher and Nathan into this. It seemed he wouldn't have a choice. They were the only two he would trust.

Without another word to Garrett, he turned away and pulled his phone out of his pocket. It rang several times before he answered.

"Hello?" Asher answered, and it surprised Zachary how much he'd needed to talk to him.

"Hey."

"Zachary." Rustling sounded through the speaker and a quick gasp. Asher and Gwen must be in bed.

"I'm coming back and I need to meet with you. Nathan too."

"When?" Asher must have heard in his tone what Zachary was calling for. His single word answer was short and alert.

"A day, two at the most."

"We'll be ready." No question, no hesitation. And this was why Zachary couldn't have told Asher what had happened to Holly or where he was going. Asher would help him no matter what, putting his life, and Gwen's life, in danger. Putting Kai in danger and leaving Smoke without those that were important to him once again. Zachary didn't have a choice. He wouldn't trust anyone else.

He hung up and turned to Garrett. "I'm not bringing them in until we know what we're doing. Let's start planning."

ZACHARY INHALED, letting the smell of home invade his body. The fresh air weaved through his fur, bringing his soul up from the depths of his core. He hadn't realized how irritated he felt being in a city.

The framework and roof of the safe house Asher was building was half finished and looking great. At the front sat a bag with his name written on a piece of paper and stapled to it. He walked over and nudged it with his nose. Asher's scent rose from the clothes inside.

Running snapped his attention up. A white wolf appeared and tackled Smoke to the ground, who's tail had been wagging furiously. They tumbled and rolled, growling and yipping. Several minutes later, they stopped and touched their heads together while panting. Their connection hit Zachary hard. Family. Pack. Jealousy roared with an ugly snarl. He had to shut it down. Smoke needed the pack. Zachary just hoped that soon, Smoke would include him as pack.

Turning away from the wolves, Zachary shifted and put on the clothes Asher left for him. In the bag, he also found a cell phone. After turning it on, he found Asher's, Nathan's, and his phone numbers programmed inside. He tapped on Asher's name and waited. A single ring and he answered.

"You're here."

"I am."

"We'll be right there."

Zachary walked around the building to see the progress they'd made while he'd been in the city. Asher was doing a great job. A great determination formed in his chest. He wanted to finish this, bring his girls home. He wanted to create a home. A home of his own. Envious of Asher and

Nathan, Zachary realized that was what he'd wanted all along. Smoke finding Kai's pack was the best thing that ever happened to them. It would still take time for Zachary and Smoke to finish healing the damage, and it wouldn't come without frustrations, but they'd be doing it with a home, a family, a pack.

The sounds of two sets of racing paws echoed toward him. One quick and light, the other spaced out thumps. A grizzly and a white wolf came to a stop outside of the building. Zachary stepped out and saw each had a woman on their backs. Gwen and Shaye slid off the animals to allow them to shift.

A rush of warmth filled the space, taking away the nip from the chilly air for only a moment, as the white and brown winds circled the animals, the magic that helped shifters change.

Once as men, they walked toward the building. Asher hunched down and pulled out a duffel bag from under the temporary front steps. He tossed jeans and a t-shirt to Nathan and then pulled out a set for himself.

"Glad to see you back." Asher finished pulling his shirt over his head. Nathan only stared, the deep brown of his eyes motionless. Zachary didn't blame the guy for not being friendly. Not with the way they last parted.

"I'm not back for long."

Asher moved to stand beside Gwen, and Shaye tucked herself against Nathan.

"This is looking good." Zachary gestured to the building behind him.

"Stop stalling." Nathan's words didn't hold anger, but he wasn't willing to wait. Zachary sighed. Guess it was finally his turn to tell all.

"The day that I first shifted, our neighbour, my mother's

cousin, had a baby, a little girl. I grew attached, more than just attached. She became a little sister. I spent time with her daily. The day after her eighth birthday, they moved away from Hull Creek. We planned to keep in touch, but it was no more than a few phone calls over the first few years. Something I'll forever regret. A little over two years ago, I got a call from my parents saying Holly was missing. Didn't take long and they discovered she'd been taken. I went into a rage to search for her."

"That's when you were separated from Smoke," Gwen said, her sweet nature gentling the words, but she wasn't saying the truth.

"I'd abandoned him. Not on purpose, but I ran off without telling him first and bringing him along. I wasn't thinking and I should have. That's on me." Smoke walked over and nudged his hip hard enough to make him step sideways to catch his balance. The grey wolf huffed at him, then sat down, his tail swatting at debris in the grass.

"I take it you've found her?" Nathan eyed him, all the pieces falling into place behind his eyes.

"Yeah. Damien's organization supplied many of the girls. He took her. That's why I had worked my way in with him to find where he sent them. I thought I was close."

"Supplied girls for what?" Asher's protective nature roared in his quiet words and his eyes flashed bright.

"The last night I was here, and the woman appeared, she told me where to find Holly. It's taken some time to get in, but I have, with some help. It's a fighting ring. Of women only."

"Fuck." Asher cursed low and closed his eyes. Shaye's hands drifted over Nathan's arm in front of her.

"There's more." He waited for them to calm. "Holly's a shifter, an owl. She changed after she moved."

"Do they know what she is?" asked Nathan.

"No. There's another shifter in there too. A hawk. The same hawk we spotted here a few months ago. He's the doctor of the organization, but not part of it. They blackmailed him, but he never left." It would be up to Garrett to tell about his sister and rest of his story.

"Why?"

"He wouldn't abandon the rest of the girls. He's the one helping me. But we need more help for our plan to work. I didn't want to ask. I didn't want to involve any of you. It puts you, your families, and everything Asher is trying to build in danger. So you need to say no if this is too much. But you two are the only ones I trust." It all spewed from his mouth before he could stop himself. He came here to ask for their help. Zachary wouldn't push them away now that he was here.

"Are the police an option?" Shaye asked.

"We couldn't do this our way with police involved, needing to watch what we say and do so as not to give away what we are." Asher and Nathan nodded firmly with Zachary's explanation.

"I'm in." Asher's eyes still flashed with the animal's instincts.

"Me too." Nathan pulled Shaye tighter and lifted his head.

"Thank you." Zachary didn't intend to growl. "There's one more thing."

"What is it?" Nathan looked ready for whatever was about to happen.

"My mate is in there too."

CHAPTER 9

It'd been days since they'd seen Zachary or talked to the doctor. They wouldn't allow him to see them without a reason, however he sent imperceptible nods their way when passing on the club floor. But Zachary had been absent.

"We'll know it when it happens." Holly gave the reassurance each night with a flat tone. She didn't believe her own words. Ezaray's eyes stung as she continued to grip the thought of escape, and Zachary.

Tonight's fight pulled in a large crowd. One that would gain many bets for both fighters. Holly versus Maggie. The only reason Holly would win would be because of her increased strength as a shifter. As fighters, they both fought well, having equal skill. It could be anyone's win. Ezaray expected an edgy crowd.

And it was. As she stopped on her rounds, men got themselves into a debate on the anticipated winner. Ezaray's stomach rolled with each disgusting word.

Holly would hate to defeat Maggie, but she'd have no choice. Tyrone had been watching her ever since her last fight. He'd taken over for Gerard on several training sessions. Having him that close set them both on edge.

Tyrone had made it clear what would happen to Holly if he caught her pulling punches again. It would be uncharacteristic of him to follow through on that with one of his best fighters, but he'd yet to go back on a promise for the two plus years Ezaray had been here. She wouldn't put any bet on that changing now.

Ezaray caught up to Holly, dressed for her fight and shaking. Tremors ran down her limbs. Ezaray hadn't seen Holly scared since the day they arrived here. But that only meant Holly refused to show it before now.

"What am I going to do, Zee? I can't put Maggie's life in danger. I can't do it." Holly's hand slid down Ezaray's arm and gripped her wrist. They stood side by side, hiding the gesture. "But Tyrone will catch me. I don't know if I can hide it well enough."

"Maggie's the top fighter next to you. She's not in danger by losing one fight."

"I'm not so sure about that." Holly's voice took on an eerie sound. "Something's up with Tyrone." She led them through the men, gently steering away from ones that might look like they wanted to talk. Their club floor faces never faltered, despite the fear flowing off Holly. "I have no idea what it is. I can't explain it." Her voice caught. "I wish Zachary was here."

It was the first real thing Holly had said in a long time. Ezaray used her opposite hand to reach across her front and squeeze Holly's wrist, not caring if anyone noticed the gesture. For once, Ezaray needed to be strong for Holly.

"Deep breath, Holly. Everything will be fine."

"It won't," she argued, but took the breath anyway. They kept walking and avoiding the men, ending their rounds early. As soon as they reached the back of the room, the rest of girls made their way over, assuming they could finish their rounds as well. Ezaray had to pry Holly's hand from her wrist.

"Don't do this now. You've got this, Holly."

Holly returned with a solid nod while the rest of her body still quaked. She and Maggie left toward the locker room while the rest waited in the back until it was time to go back out to take bets.

Tyrone didn't waste time tonight. The doors swung open only five minutes later, allowing them out.

Ezaray couldn't focus. She walked the room and placed bets on her tablet with the motions engraved in her memory. This wasn't part of the job she dared rush. If they missed out on taking bets, Tyrone would be furious. As the time dragged on, she made her way around the room as her dread increased. Holly's words got to her. Ezaray searched the room for Tyrone, wanting to see for herself if there was something wrong with him. But she didn't find him.

Reaching the back of the room, Ezaray sighed as the door was in sight. They'd make their way to the seating stage to watch the fight.

Three steps from the door, she had an urge to turn. Looking to her right, silver eyes warmed her skin. Zachary was back. She wanted to run to him. To feel his touch and what little safety he provided. He closed his eyes and his muscles tensed for a moment. When he opened them again, the swirling brightness had dimmed.

Zachary nodded at Ezaray, a nod with a purpose, saying words he couldn't. Tonight was it. They were escaping tonight.

Anxiety flared and tingled along her skin. She walked through the back doors feeling useless and unprepared. It was all up to Zachary. She was either looking at her last day of captivity or the day everything would go terribly wrong.

Ezaray followed the line of girls to the seating stage. She didn't want to watch this fight. No matter the outcome, both Holly and Maggie would be in pain. Hopefully, neither in pain at the hands of Tyrone.

Men cheered as the two walked out of the locker rooms. Holly's face lifted for a moment before she lowered it to the ground again. She must have smelled Zachary. Ezaray hoped that helped steady her.

They stepped into the ring and Tyrone followed them in and stood in the centre with his signature microphone. "Gentlemen, tonight will be a treat, I guarantee it. I know tonight was a tough choice for placing your bets, but win or lose, it will be an epic evening." He paused while his eyes roamed the room. The silence amped up the anticipation, a thick cloud hovering over all the heads. "Fight!" Tyrone boomed and stepped back just as the bell dinged.

Holly and Maggie stepped toward the centre. Ezaray had to turn away. She looked down and to the side and closed her eyes. The sounds of the fight filtered through the cheering of the crowd. She cringed, not sure if she could take only listening for much longer when the bell rang for the end of the first round.

Ezaray looked up. Holly and Maggie were in almost identical shape. She searched for Tyrone, who watched from just outside the ring. His face was murderous. Her body chilled at the sight of his black eyes. Holly was right. There was something going on with Tyrone. But did it have to do with Holly? He'd been on her since her last fight. And right now, those black eyes were staring at her. Whatever Zachary had planned, it needed to happen soon.

She looked across the room where she'd last seen him, but he wasn't there.

The bell rang and the fight continued. This time, Ezaray didn't look away. She watched Holly to be sure she wasn't giving Tyrone a reason to kill her. She wasn't. Maggie was good enough to keep her on her toes. But Tyrone's eyes narrowed on Holly. He must not believe it.

The fight dragged on; the crowd became frustrated. Tyrone rang the bell for the end of the match and stepped into the ring. He didn't say a word as he grabbed Holly's wrist and held it in the air. A mix of cheers and growls rolled over the room before they all quieted as Tyrone didn't move.

Then the smile that crept up the side of his face scared the air from Ezaray's chest. Whatever he was about to say as he lifted his microphone wouldn't be good.

"Tonight is the night where you all take a vote." He released Holly's wrist. "You pick your favourite fighter and your least favourite fighter. The handlers will come around to discuss shortly. In the meantime..." Tyrone trailed off, his head and shoulders turning to eye the seating stage with the rest of the fighters. "We have a treat for you."

A security guard opened the stage door. He pointed to the girl closest to him and pulled out a set of hand wraps from a black bag hanging off his opposite hand.

He wouldn't. Tyrone cherished the health of his fighters. Ezaray looked back at the stage. Tyrone was talking to the doctor who had a hand on Maggie, leading her out of the ring. The doctor nodded and took Maggie to his exam room. As he passed the seating stage, his face was hard and unreadable.

The security guard had Tina by the elbow and was pulling her toward the stage.

"I have a theory to test, gentlemen, and in doing so,

you're going to see a lot of fights. If you don't yet know who your favourite fighters are, you soon will." Tyrone stepped out of the ring, leaving Holly there. Holly was in the same shape as Maggie and Tyrone still expected her to fight.

The guard pushed Tina into the ring. As the excitement grew across the crowd, the bell rang and the two fighters stepped up.

After the bell for the first round, the doctor let a bandaged-up Maggie in to sit with the rest of them. Then he made his way back to the stage, his shoulders straight and tense and his steps purposeful. The second fight ended quickly, and they passed Tina down to the doctor.

The guard was back and pointed to Lesley sitting next to Ezaray. Holly couldn't make it through everyone. She was good, but not that good. She wasn't unbeatable. This would break her.

Her fight with Lesley lasted longer than Tina's. Just as the doctor returned Tina, the fight had ended.

An ominous weight fell on Ezaray as the guard pointed at her. It wasn't the first time she had to fight against Holly, but this felt different. Nothing about tonight was normal. She tried to blank her mind and treat this like any other fight rather than against her weakened best friend. This fight would last a lot longer than the first two. Holly wasn't yet weak enough that Ezaray could beat her quickly, but it was likely she would win in the end.

As usual she kept her head high and her features emotionless. But inside she cried.

ZACHARY COULDN'T LEAVE, but he had to. Disgust at his form of abandonment choked him as his feet pulled him along.

Keeping his head up and his face blank was difficult. If he stayed, if he saw Holly take another hit, he'd lose his control. His skin crawled like waves as he fought off his inner wolf. He reached the end of the ring and froze. The scent that filled his nose forced him to shut his eyes before they glowed bright silver.

His mate was in the ring.

He changed his direction toward the bar as if that had been his intention. He ordered a drink and hoped the action would focus him enough from shifting. If he felt himself losing control again, he'd have to leave Holly and Ezaray.

They needed to hold on for a few more hours. They were getting them out of here tonight.

More than the basic sounds of a fight reached his ears. They were over sensitive with a shift so close to the surface. He heard the grunts and moans coming from each of the girls. A whimper he recognized from a small Holly. Zachary gritted his teeth. Sharp breaths came from Ezaray.

The crowd broke out in a mix of emotions, the scents of each flooding his nose. Zachary turned around. Holly lay on the floor on her stomach, trying to push herself back up. Ezaray looked down at her with her arms lowered. Holly's elbows gave out and she collapsed. Tyrone stepped forward and raised Ezaray's arm.

The chaos of the crowd drowned out Zachary's growl toward the man touching his mate.

A security guard stepped into the ring and lifted Holly over to Garrett, who carried her to the back.

A few deep breaths and Zachary calmed, but as they let another girl into the ring, he saw Tyrone's plan. Each girl would fight until they couldn't anymore. None of the girls could help with the escape tonight.

Time to step up their plan.

Zachary left. He hated himself for leaving his mate while she still fought, but he needed to give Tyrone a reason to cut this short.

He sent a text to Asher before he got in the elevator to move closer to the main entrance. Their plan was a subtle one. Give Tyrone a reason to believe he was being watched. The three of them had been taking turns for the past several days watching the place, ensuring they were seen, but not recognized. Putting pressure on Tyrone to move. Zachary had been happy to hear whispers from the guards tonight. Tyrone knew he was being watched.

When he reached the front doors, Asher and Nathan were parked directly across the street. Zachary lifted his hand off the door and turned around. He stared at the guard by the elevator until the air in the room changed, until the guard realized there were eyes on him. The guard glared back, but frowned when Zachary nodded his head out the door. The guard didn't move. Zachary shrugged and walked through, swinging the door wide so the front of the car would be visible while the door was open.

He knew the guard spotted Asher and Nathan when he heard steps rushing behind him. The guard caught the door before it shut. Hopefully, the added pressure of being watched would cut Tyrone's fun short.

EVERY MUSCLE ACHED. Ezaray fought the last two girls that the guard brought out, and won, but not without taking a lot of hits. After a guard spoke into Tyrone's ear, his face hardened as he cut off the guard fetching the fighters. He quickly ended the evening and sent the patrons away with promises of the season's ending.

The doctor rushed through treating each of them. As he finished treating Ezaray, Tyrone stepped into his office, something he never did.

"Send her back upstairs. You're dismissed for the rest of the night." The cords down his neck ticked and his knuckles were white while squeezing the handle of the door. Something had agitated Tyrone. His hair was loose although still held in the elastic at the back of his head. A permanently stamped crease held his brows down.

If he was ever anything but calm, they needed to worry. His dismissal of the doctor made little sense to her, taking away their healer after so many fought tonight.

"Understood." The doctor nodded. When Tyrone left, he turned back to Ezaray. His jaw locked. "Be ready."

Ezaray swallowed to hold down any excitement. The emotional pain would hurt worse than the physical pain she had now if their plan failed.

The doctor helped her off the exam table and escorted her to the elevator. He would have followed her in and helped her to her room, but the guard stopped him, reminding the doctor Tyrone had dismissed him.

Ezaray rode the elevator alone and quietly let herself into their room so she didn't disturb Holly. She hovered over Holly who lay motionless in her bed, her breathing steady. Bruises had formed over her weak body. Ezaray knew she was in the same shape, but enough adrenaline ran through her knowing they were getting out soon. But not knowing how they were escaping terrified her.

She sat on the side of Holly's bed, her head falling forward. Jerking up, she pulled in a deep breath. She needed to stay awake, stay alert. She wasn't successful. Dozing in and out of consciousness, Ezaray lost track of the time. Quick thumping sounded in the hall.

Ezaray gently shook Holly, hoping she'd wake up.

"Holly. Something's happening."

Holly blinked and groaned as she tried to sit up. Their door opened. Gerard and Maggie's handler stood there. A security guard with them held a weak and bruised Maggie by her elbow.

"Get up. We're leaving."

"Leaving?" asked Holly with a groggy croak.

"Don't get excited." Gerard sneered. "There's a new home already waiting for you."

Ezaray stood and reached down to help Holly. Not that she had the strength to be a help. They walked past Gerard and into the hall, still in their bare feet. Shoes and socks weren't a luxury they gave them, ever.

She held in her moan when Gerard took her arm to make her move faster. They pushed them through the hall toward the elevator. Holly stumbled once, but the guard roughly pulled her back to her feet, keeping a hand on her until she caught up with their steps. Ezaray wanted to reach for her, but couldn't.

Behind them, each bedroom door had a waiting handler and guard. Ezaray was shoved to face forward again. They kept the three of them apart, a man between each of them as they rode the elevator down.

They reached the back exit of the building, one Ezaray had never seen before. The guard pushed on the door, but the scratch of a radio stopped him.

"Hold," a muffled voice came out the small black radio hanging on his belt. He pulled the door closed and waited.

This had to be it. This had to be when Zachary planned to get them out.

CHAPTER 10

They'd put the pressure on Tyrone and started the rumours inside the building. Asher and Nathan moved closer each day until tonight when Zachary signalled them again. They changed clothes and vehicles every other day to make it look like a whole team was watching the building. Security had been on edge and it became obvious that night that something crawled beneath Tyrone's skin.

Garrett said he'd been kicked out until further notice. It happened every time they moved. The mega tournament Tyrone had suddenly created however, wasn't normal and weighed on Zachary's mind. He wanted to know its purpose. But there was no time to find out, and it wouldn't matter after tonight, anyway.

Everything from fear to anticipation coursed through Zachary. His muscles tensed and his heart rate kicked, ready to dance, ready to inflict pain on those that deserved it most. The noises of the city grated on his over-alert senses. Cars, horns, sirens, and people screaming and hollering. It all annoyed him.

Movement at the front door drew his attention. His eyes

hyper-focused on the two security guards, one dressed to match Tyrone's clothes, but it wasn't Tyrone. Zachary smirked at their attempt at a diversion.

He nodded across the street at Asher and Nathan still sitting in the car. His way of telling them to follow along. Tyrone wanted to lose the tail before he or the girls moved. They needed him to believe he had.

As Nathan pulled their car out after the guards, their headlights out, Zachary stalked toward the back of the building. Moments after the cars disappeared, Tyrone and two guards stepped out the back to a waiting SUV. Important man he thought he was.

It was difficult to let him go, but they'd decided they couldn't get him and save the girls. Most of the men that worked or profited under him wouldn't get out of this. Zachary hoped one of the weasels had enough desire to save their own ass they'd roll on Tyrone. It would give him some peace of mind once he got the girls home.

Zachary hesitated before going back to the front of the building. If he were Tyrone, he'd continue to have decoys out the front and bring the girls out the back. He had enough guys for it. He'd at least have a spotter out front. A spotter. Zachary looked up to the roof and pointed to the front of the building. Garrett spread his wings and swooped across the street. When he came back, he nodded.

Garrett didn't want to be seen by any of the guards or handlers. If things didn't go right, he still wanted to be there for the girls in the new place. It left them to do this with three men. One at the moment, until Asher and Nathan got back.

Zachary signalled for Garrett to get to the ground. He flew down with a silent, graceful swoop, landing on the fire escape of the building beside Tyrone's in the alley.

"We need a distraction. Something for the spotter to make them wait. We need to stall until Asher and Nathan get back. I can't take out the spotter and whoever has the girls."

Garrett flew off, up high, then back across the street. A crash emanated from the darkness in the opposite alley, just as the back door opened. It closed quickly as he heard the front door open and saw the spotter step out onto the sidewalk. Another crash. The spotter crossed the street. As he looked left to right, Garrett emerged into the air and perched on the building to spy down into the alley. The back door remained closed.

Come on. He needed Asher and Nathan.

The spotter came back across the street and lifted his radio to his mouth. Zachary heard the fuzzy crack and the faint "Clear." The back door opened as Asher and Nathan slammed themselves against the side of the building.

"Thank fuck. Get the spotter. Silently. Don't damage the radio. We might need it." He spoke fast, the urgency of the change in plans spiking his whisper.

Nathan ran to the front, and Asher and Zachary watched two handlers and a security guard with three women between them. The red hair stood out in the dark and the scents of the other two were clear in his system. Maggie, Ezaray, and Holly were coming out at once and with three escorts. Fuck. He hoped Nathan didn't take long or that one of the girls would be capable of helping.

Zachary and Asher skulked after them on silent feet through the shadows until they reached a small parking lot of cars behind the next building. The guard's hand left his pocket after the black SUV's lights blinked and the short beep of the locking mechanism echoed off the other cars.

He was the only one alert. Zachary saw the tiny twitch of

his head as Asher closed the distance behind him. The guard spun Maggie, throwing her against the car, and in the same motion, he swung a fist back that connected with Asher's jaw. Damn. That had to hurt, but Asher never lost his footing.

Zachary managed an instant grip around the tallest of the handlers. One arm around the guy's neck bent at a small angle to cut off circulation and the other hand grabbed the wrist holding onto Ezaray and squeezed, the bones inside beginning to crush forcing him to let go. Faint footfalls approached as the guy under his arm slid to the ground. Zachary whirled around with relief at seeing Nathan joining them. He helped Asher get the guard down in short order.

Zachary turned to take on the other handler, but Holly was already on his shoulders, the changing colours of his face visible even in the dark as she squeezed with her thighs. Zachary reached out and caught her off his shoulders as he fell to the ground.

"I've got you, Squirt." Zachary took only a second to hold her and lean his forehead against hers. They weren't finished yet. The entire fight took only seconds, and they needed to move the car and secure the guard and handlers. He set Holly on the ground and kept himself from grabbing Ezaray. Looking over the girls, they were fine except for the bruising and soreness from their fights.

"Are they all coming out in threes?" Nathan helped Maggie off the car, checking her shoulders and back. She shook her head.

"I don't think so." Ezaray's voice was airy, shaky.

"I've got the car." Asher pulled the keys from the guard's pocket and reached for the door.

"Hey," Zachary called to Asher. He turned around. "You

should have seen that coming." Zachary let his lip curl up to tease the man.

Asher rolled his eyes. "Fuck off." But Zachary saw him smiling as he got in the SUV and slowly drove it away.

"Holly, Ezaray, and Maggie, back that way to the shadows. Get out of sight. We'll show you where our cars are." Zachary couldn't hold back from running his hand down Ezaray's arm. He didn't have time to do what he wanted, and he didn't know how she'd react. Ezaray and Maggie watched the ground as they jogged back on their bare feet.

"I'm helping." Holly lifted her stubborn chin.

"You're hurt."

"I'm better than I look. I'm helping." She bent down to drag the shorter handler away. Nathan had the other over his shoulder. Zachary didn't have time to argue. He bent and lifted the guard. He went back and helped Holly after he dumped him in the alley.

"Holly, did anyone clear you to leave over the radio?"

"No. They only spoke when not to leave, then cleared us."

"Good. Now we need to hurry."

Asher came back just as they finished securing the three guys and helped deposit them inside the dumpster with the spotter. RCMP would find them in one convenient spot later tonight.

The three girls huddled together against the wall. He stepped in front of them. "We have our own waiting cars." Zachary looked up. Garrett swooped down. Wide eyes glowed dimly from Ezaray and Maggie. "Follow the hawk."

"I told you, I'm helping." Holly's nostrils flared. It was an expression he'd seen on her countless time, although it used to be followed by a foot stomping.

"Okay. We need you to help get the girls out of there and over here. If we need you for the fight, then I'll tell you."

Holly nodded.

"Go with them so you can take the rest of the girls to the cars too." All three followed Garrett as he flew low through between the concrete buildings.

Zachary's entire body itched to follow Ezaray, but he, Asher, and Nathan turned back into the shadows to wait for the next pair to walk out the door.

DISBELIEF SEARED HER HEART. They were free. Ezaray sat with Maggie in the back of one vehicle while Holly showed the rest of the girls back in pairs. The hawk, the doctor she assumed, had gone out of sight after first showing them back here. They weren't far from the building, but around enough corners that no one would associate the cars with what was happening.

Time stretched and the silence eerie as they kept waiting for Holly to bring back the next pair. Guilt settled in a little nest inside Ezaray. Holly was helping. She should be too, but she couldn't. Holly must have already begun to heal. Every part of Ezaray had turned numb, the ache in her limbs weighed her down. Now that she no longer worried over Holly, the energy left her muscles. The warmth poured out of them like a slow downward stream, leaving behind a chill. Maggie was the same, holding back her shivers as they sat shoulder to shoulder.

Ezaray turned her head. Two more girls followed Holly. She put them in another car then came over to theirs, opening the back door.

"One more run. The guards and handlers are still unconscious. I don't know what their plan is for them. You two still good?" Holly sounded in control of herself.

"We're good. Do you need any help?" Ezaray didn't have the strength, but she offered anyway. Holly was doing what she did best, take care of others.

"We have it covered out there, but blue eyes said there were blankets in the trunk of this car. Can you get them out and pass them around?"

"Of course." Eager to find warmth, Ezaray slid across the seat and out the door Holly held open. Holly ran back and Ezaray stepped to the back to open the hatch door. She took three of the blankets and passed them to Maggie for them to keep in that car, then took four to the girls in the other car and the rest to the SUV in the back of the line. No one said a word, but they hastily grabbed the blankets and started wrapping themselves. Ezaray went back to her car and wrapped herself up beside Maggie.

The blanket wasn't enough. The fear of what would happen next tried to choke her. Where were they going to take all of them? The car closed in around her. She turned to reach for the handle to escape the metal trap and saw Holly coming back with the last two girls. She helped them into the last car, that was almost full, and then hopped in beside Ezaray, blocking her in the middle of the back seat. Holly didn't reach for the blanket. She only sat on the edge of the seat and looked at Ezaray and Maggie. Her eyes darted back to Ezaray, reading the panic on her face.

"It's okay, Zee." Holly clasped Ezaray's hand between hers and held on, but only until the guys came into view. A sad half smile appeared on Holly's face. Leaning forward, she placed a gentle kiss on Ezaray's cheek. "Love you, Zee."

Ezaray stared at Holly as she got out of the car. Zachary grabbed her shoulders to stop her. Their words turned heated and Holly wrenched herself from his grasp. With slow steps backward, Holly shook her head at Zachary. Then she turned and ran.

If Ezaray hadn't been staring after her, she wouldn't have seen the doctor step from the shadows and run after her. She could only see Zachary's back, but his body shrunk.

THEY THREW ALL the men in the dumpster. Not comfortably either. Just how they should be. It was a pile of unconscious weight lying on top of each other at odd angles. They left a piece of cardboard on top with the words *IN HERE* written on it. Nathan lifted his phone to his ear and gave all the details to an anonymous tip line. RCMP would be here any minute. They ran to their own waiting cars.

As he approached his, the one that held Holly and his mate, Holly stepped out and tried to run past him.

"Where are you going?" He gripped her shoulders.

"I'm leaving. I'm free."

"You're coming home with me."

"I need to find my owl." Her voice frantic and her body shook in a way he was all too familiar with. He felt the magic heating her skin.

"Holly, a shift is going to hurt. You're still injured." He tried to pull her to him, to hold her and help her fight off the change until he could get her somewhere safe.

"Don't care, Zachary."

"Holly. Squirt."

"I'm not her anymore!" She wrenched herself out of his hands.

"Alder Ridge. Go to Alder Ridge. Please." His demand was really begging. He wanted to bring her home.

She backed away. Garrett's voice called with a low hum from the shadows, still staying out of sight of the girls.

"Your owl pair spends a lot of time on the roof of the building." Of course the hawk would have known that.

Holly turned and ran away. The pain in his chest was sharp. He'd promised he'd get her home. His foot moved forward to chase her, but he remembered he had fourteen other girls to get to safety too. He didn't want to admit it, but Holly could take care of herself. He'd made sure of it when they were kids.

Zachary stared after her, Garrett following. He saw the winds rush around the corner, two colours, then he watched the sky. An owl and a hawk soared upward and disappeared on the roof of the building from which they were both free. When he heard the faint screeches of owls, he turned toward the cars.

Asher and Nathan were waiting by the driver's doors. Their eyes held sympathy, but he wasn't sure if it was for him or Holly. He got in the car and wanted to say something, but nothing came out. Giving Ezaray and Maggie a reassuring nod, he started the car and drove off.

All three spread out, taking adjacent routes to get to the motel.

"Where's Holly? Why didn't we wait for her?" Ezaray's voice squeaked and quaked. Zachary glanced at her through the rearview mirror. Holly said Ezaray knew what she was. "She didn't want us to wait for her, did she?"

"No." He chanced a look over at Maggie. Her brows scrunched together, but she didn't ask what they all really wanted to know. Where did she go? To the roof under the power of her own wings. But after she reunited with her pair, he didn't know what she'd planned. He hoped Garrett stayed with her until she was somewhere safe, even bring her home to Alder Ridge. Alder Ridge wasn't her home, but it was his now. He'd get her to her parents, when she was ready. When he was ready.

He pulled into the motel with Asher and Nathan joining only seconds behind him. They'd already booked the rooms and all three of them had keys.

Opening the back door, he offered a hand to help Maggie out. Graciously, she took it. As Asher and Nathan led the other girls toward the room, he nudged Maggie in that direction and helped Ezaray out. He shut her door and looked down at her. He didn't think he kept his eyes from flashing based on how warm they felt. She didn't pull away in fear.

Zachary erupted. He crushed Ezaray against his chest and held on tight. He'd trapped her hands between their bodies, but she laid her cheek on him. Her sweet cherry scent drifted up and filled his senses.

Nathan calling his name forced him to pull away. He closed his eyes to dispel the animal's gaze.

"We need to get inside."

Ezaray nodded and padded over the pavement with her still bare feet.

Inside, the girls were all gathered on the beds and Asher and Nathan had been waiting for Zachary to take over. He'd hoped Asher would have stepped up. He would have been more gentle with them.

"We haven't taken you away from one hell to throw you into another. You're all free. We'll get you all home or wherever it is you want to go." Zachary looked at each of them, then landed on Ezaray. Home. He just promised to take Ezaray home, to her home. He couldn't do it, not yet. "I don't know where Tyrone is or how many guys he has left. The RCMP should be picking up all the men that were with you as we speak, and the RCMP will be on Tyrone's trail. But I can't say what he'll do next. You all need to know that. We have this room and the one next door for the night. Take turns showering, sleeping, whatever you need. We'll get information from each of you and start getting you home."

"We have bags of clothes here that you're all welcome to have." Asher showed them the bags sitting in the cubby closet then they started talking to each of the girls to find out where they were from. Zachary only had one of them on his mind.

He held his hand out to Ezaray, pleased when she took it. Pulling her up, he sat her in one of the side chairs and pushed it close to its pair. Zachary sat and faced her, setting his hands on the outsides of her knees.

"I'm sure you want to go home to your family. But I want you to come home with me." It was difficult not to demand her, and yet he still didn't say it as a request.

"We need to find Holly." She leaned forward in her seat, her eyes boring into him, begging him to find her friend.

"I'm hoping she'll show up in Alder Ridge. Or that Garrett will bring her there." If he had been in her shoes, with wings, he'd be in the skies, the trees, far above land and man. There was no way for a wolf to find her until she was ready.

"Who's Garrett?" She looked across the room to the other two men, then out the window.

"The doctor."

"Finally, a name." Her lips twitched, but the amusement died. "You're not going to go try to find her? You came here for her, didn't you?"

"I did. I found her and I found you. You know what she is. I won't be able to find her until she's ready. But Garrett followed her."

"Holly said the doctor is a hawk." Seems Holly had opened up in their last days there.

"That's right."

"And you're a wolf?" Her tone dropped to a whisper, and she tried to hide her shake, but her lips still quivered until she flattened them. Zachary inhaled, trying to sense her emotions, to separate them from the adrenaline from the escape. Nervous, but no fear.

"Yes."

"And what about them?" Small sea-green eyes darted toward Asher then Nathan.

"A wolf and a bear." The blanket tightened around her shoulders and her eyes came down to her lap. White teeth pulled in her plump bottom lip and worked it back and forth. "Ezaray."

Her gaze lifted, filled with trust he hadn't yet earned.

"Come home with me." No question. He needed her too much to give her a choice.

"Okay."

"Thank fuck." He wouldn't argue with how easy she agreed. He would accept what Fate handed him.

CHAPTER 11

A handful of girls broke down and wanted to go home right away. Their families lived close and the guy with Zachary, the one that always scowled, drove them home. That left nine of them to share the beds in the two rooms for the night. They took turns showering and changing into the baggy sweats the guys bought for them, saving the leggings and nicer tunics for going home. All brand new.

Tyrone had got them clothes, but only t-shirts and shorts aside from the uniforms they wore on the floor. Receiving new clothes like this was different. It may not have been meant as a gift, but that's exactly what it felt like. And it made her feel just little bit special.

She pulled the collar of her sweater to her nose and inhaled. The clothes smelled new.

Zachary sat in the chair to the side of the window, watching the parking lot outside. Why had she agreed to go with him? She should go home to her mom and brother. She should at least be out looking for Holly first, and they both could go home together.

He was the hero of them all, but when he touched her, looked at her, said her name, a bed of embers grew and heated inside her. His mussed hair fell over narrowed eyes, eyes that she'd seen glow. The shadow on his jaw and around his mouth had gotten darker. A wolf hiding beneath the man should concern her. She understood about Holly, but Holly was only an owl. Zachary, and his friends, were large predators. Yet, they showed an interest in rescuing them, all of them, when no one else who'd entered that place had.

There'd been a pull toward Zachary inside the club, but now that she was free of those restraints, she only felt confused. Floundering in a world she no longer knew. Ezaray needed to go to her family, but she didn't want to see people. She didn't want to face the world, and she didn't want to face home without Holly.

Zachary was a bold choice set in front of her, giving her a reason to hide.

He didn't treat any of the other girls the same way he'd treated her. Like an attraction he didn't know what to do about it.

Oh, she bet he knew what to do about it. Her situation made him pause.

Blue eyes, as Holly had pegged him, stepped into the room. It surprised Ezaray how silently such big men could move. She only heard him, and saw him, because she'd been awake.

"Nathan's back too. He's patrolling outside."

Zachary nodded, his eyes never left the parking lot.

"I'll take a turn at the window."

Zachary didn't argue, and Asher took his place. But as soon as his focus was off watching for danger, it turned directly on her. He crouched down on her side of the bed so his face was level with hers.

"You're the only one not asleep." He'd known that whole time without ever looking at her.

"Too much to think about, I guess."

"You need to stop thinking, just for tonight. Get some sleep."

She expected he'd stand up and leave her, but he lifted his hand. One callused finger traced a line down her nose, then over her brow to circle her eye. He repeated the motions. The slow, steady strokes calmed her body, releasing tension she clung to. Her eyes drifted closed, but she fought it. His silver eyes in front of her looked past everything she had to her soul. But what he might see there scared her. She didn't even know what of her soul still existed.

"You're thinking again." He lulled her with a shushing sound. Again, her eyes drifted. When she fought them open, Zachary slowly shook his head. Ezaray let go of the fight.

She closed her eyes and allowed sleep to take her. Her last thought was that in that moment, she knew she'd made the right choice to go home with Zachary.

ZACHARY HAD SLEPT TOO. He surprised himself, but once Ezaray slept soundly, exhaustion forced his eyelids shut. They'd taken turns throughout the night to watch, one inside and one outside, and always checking on both rooms.

Faint light was barely visible with the sunrise beginning in the distance. All three men were up and ready, but the girls still slept. Four were from a town five hours away. Asher offered to take that drive. Maggie still hadn't told them where she was from. She hadn't said a word to any of them. Nathan would try this morning to get her to talk, or see if she'd talk to Ezaray. And Ezaray would come home with Zachary.

He'd be stupid not to fear what Tyrone would do now that he'd lost his business and a large chunk of his men to go with it. But his focus right now would be on his mate.

They all wanted to be home today, so they woke the girls.

"Time to take you home." Asher crouched down rather than stood over the girls while they readjusted to their surroundings. Zachary brushed Ezaray's hair out of her face and squeezed her shoulder.

"Wake up, lovely."

Her eyes fluttered open and looked over the edge of the bed straight at him.

"I haven't slept like that in over two years." The awe in her groggy whisper made him hurt for her. He cursed himself for not finding them sooner, even knowing there wasn't anything he could have done. He'd been close to finding them when he'd finally gained Damien's trust. No point in dwelling on that now. They were free.

"Time to get on the road." He helped her sit up. Her face scrunched into a wince as she moved. The bruises on her face had darkened, looking worse than last night. She had to be sore and stiff. They all did.

Nathan left the other side of the bed and Maggie stood. He looked at Nathan to see him shake his head. He left the room to wake the rest of the girls next door. The last three girls' homes were about two hours away.

"Ezaray, will Maggie talk to you? We'd like to get her home, but she won't speak to any of us."

"I can try."

Zachary nodded and left her alone. Maggie was already on her way to the bathroom. Ezaray chased her in.

When they emerged, the last girl to go padded into the bathroom. They'd be ready to leave soon. Ezaray walked over while Maggie went to make the beds.

"She asked if she could come with us. She doesn't want to go home."

"Where is her home?" Zachary enjoyed Ezaray's closeness and looked down at her as she tilted her head back.

"She wouldn't say."

Part of him fostered suspicion. He had to tamp in down. If Maggie would at least talk, he might feel more reassured, but he also wouldn't leave any of them on their own after what they'd been through. "Okay. She can come with us."

Ezaray returned to Maggie, and Zachary walked over to Asher to ask if he was ready.

"Maggie's coming back with us. You guys ready?"

Nathan came back in the room and answered before Asher. "Yeah. The rest of them will be ready soon. I'll take them, then meet up with Asher on his way back. Just to make sure we don't run into anything we shouldn't."

"Not a bad idea," Zachary agreed. "I'll take Ezaray and Maggie to Alder Ridge." Zachary frowned. Alder Ridge was where he wanted to go, where Smoke was already waiting for him to return, but he didn't have his own home there. Nowhere for him to take his mate. "Well, fuck."

"What's wrong?" Asher closed off the three of them in a circle, ready for whatever problem arose.

"Nothing like that. I don't have a place to stay in Alder Ridge, not a place to take Ezaray."

"Shaye's house is still empty. I'll call her and ask her to have it ready. You three can stay there for now."

After the way they'd parted, Nathan was still helping

him. Seems Asher had worn off on the grumpy loner. "Thank you." His gratitude was a low raspy growl, but he meant it all the same.

The drive was too silent, even for him. But it was impossible to say what he wanted to say to Ezaray in front of Maggie. And they'd also have Maggie staying with them for the foreseeable future. He'd contact Shaye about house hunting for himself as soon as they got back.

Zachary looked in the rearview mirror to see Maggie hunched against the door with her knees up.

"Why don't you want to go home, Maggie?" She met his eyes in the mirror and pulled both lips together, sucking them in between her teeth. Ignoring him, she looked back out the window. "We can help if there's a reason you don't want to go. We can help you find somewhere else to go if that's what you'd prefer." She shook her head, but didn't meet his eyes in the mirror again.

What waited for her at home that would make her turn away from them after being a captive for so long? But what did Zachary know? He'd never been a captive. He'd offered to help them all, so that's what he would do. Besides, if she was a friend of his mate, then he would do everything to help.

Zachary glanced to the passenger seat. Ezaray searched everything they passed, tilting her head further to look at the sky. He had the same hopes she did, but he knew Holly wasn't up there. If she didn't show up in Alder Ridge soon, he'd go out to search for her again. But for now, he had to be satisfied that she was free.

"She'll be fine, Ezaray." This long drive would have been a great time to explain everything to Ezaray.

"I know. I'm still worried. She wasn't in a good place before the escape."

He'd thought the same. Home. They all just needed to go home. A home he intended to create.

He waited for the woman to leave before he came back to open her door and Maggie's.

EZARAY COULDN'T TAKE her eyes off the beauty of Alder Ridge as they drove into town. The town itself was a fair size, not small enough where everyone knew everyone, but landscapes and wilderness surrounded it and weaved through it. So many shades of orange, yellow, and red filled the trees. Wildflowers had grown voraciously in all that was untouched, but were coming to an end of their life cycle with the change of the season. Ezaray had always loved her beautiful home, but it didn't hold a candle to here.

Zachary pulled up to a small bungalow that sat among several others in a subdivision. In the driveway sat a black truck with a woman sitting on the tailgate. She hopped off and closed it as Zachary put the car in park.

"Stay here." Zachary squeezed her hand before getting out. Ezaray watched the two of them talk for a few minutes, then she handed Zachary a key. The woman's eyes widened in a stunned expression, then her lips twitched. Whatever Zachary had just said surprised her.

He waited for the woman to leave before he came back to open her door and Maggie's.

"Let's get you girls inside. This is where we'll be staying for a little while."

"This isn't your home?"

"No." He didn't expand and tell her where he lived. A part of her sank. She wanted to talk to him about so much, but she couldn't ask all her questions in front of Maggie. She assumed he kept his unique ability to himself as much as Holly did. Her biggest question was why he wanted her to come with him instead of going home to her family.

Zachary opened the front door and let her and Maggie go ahead of him. To the right lay a cozy living room, already furnished with a brick fireplace. A doorway that looked like it led to the kitchen opened up beside the fireplace. Straight ahead of them was a set of stairs.

"There're clothes in two of the bedrooms for both of you. She's not sure if they'll fit. If they don't, I'll get new stuff for both of you. The fridge and cupboards are stocked. The power, water, and heat are all connected, but there's no phone, TV, or Internet."

"That's okay."

"Here." He passed her a cell phone. "My number is in there. I have to go do some things, but I'll be back as soon as I can. Lock the door behind me. There's no reason to believe you're in danger here, but until I get back, don't go anywhere and don't open the door."

Maggie stepped further into the house and Zachary turned to leave, but paused, his eyes focusing on Ezaray. Panic rose inside her at being without Zachary. She didn't understand it, but being separated from him left her lonely and afraid. A hollow, airless void formed in her chest. Maggie continued into the living room and hadn't looked back at her so she wasn't showing any outward signs of panic. But it didn't escape Zachary's notice.

He faced her and stepped closer. His hands rose to her shoulders and squeezed.

"Deep breath, lovely." One hand left her shoulder and lifted her chin. "That's it." He trapped her in his eyes and she mimicked his motions without thought. "Good girl. Now, what's wrong."

"I don't want you to go." She didn't recognize her broken whisper, not all the words audible.

"I need to get rid of the car. If I didn't have to leave you, I wouldn't." One hand stayed under her chin and his other moved to tuck her hair behind her ear. His knuckles stroked over her cheek. Their bodies almost touched, but the only contact they had was his hands on her face. It felt like so much more. There was something she wasn't seeing, something she didn't understand. It had her clinging to him tighter.

"Can I come with you?"

"I want you to. So much. But stay with Maggie. Make sure she's okay. She only seems to talk to you."

He was right, and having a task, a reason to stay helped. But it wasn't enough. She couldn't pull away from him.

"Ezaray." He paused as his eyes searched her face. Then lower. Static sparked between them. A heat she'd forgotten all about rose in her core. Zachary's lips moved, but he stepped back before he did or said anything else. He caught her bottom lip with his thumb and finger. "I'll be right back."

He closed the door behind him and locked it from the outside. That didn't help her panic, but she knew she was safe. Hiding everything inside the newly formed void in her chest, she found Maggie sitting on the couch.

"Let's go check out the rooms and see if the clothes fit. Something normal would be nice."

"You're okay with all of this?" Maggie didn't indicate what *this* she was referring to.

"What do you mean?"

"Staying here, surrounded by other people. And him." She pointed at the door. "You trust him? How do you know him?"

"Holly knows him, so yes I trust him. If he says we're safe

here, then I'm okay with it." Maggie looked down to the floor and Ezaray slowly exhaled, dropping her shoulders. "I don't like being in a house in a populated neighbourhood. You're right about that. But I don't think he had much choice."

"I doubt that's true. This isn't his house."

"We're free. What more could we ask for?" Ezaray didn't care if the devil himself had rescued them, they were free to go where they wanted.

"You're right. It's just been so long." Longer for Maggie than any of them.

"I understand. Let's go upstairs."

They each found a room. Ezaray's had an attached bathroom and Maggie's was right beside the other bathroom. She took a shower, enjoying the different shampoos and facial scrubs to choose from. Drying herself off, she tried on the clothes. Some were a little snug, but found a sweater and stretchy jeans that fit enough. Maggie came out wearing a summer dress with a cardigan.

"All the pants were falling off my hips."

"They'll get us by for now. And we have the outfits from the motel. It's nice to wear something normal, even though it feels weird." Ezaray pulled at the bottom of the sweatshirt. "I'll tell Zachary when he gets back."

And with that thought, she made her way downstairs, hoping to find him waiting. But he wasn't there. Feeling lost, she went to the kitchen.

This was all too similar to her days in captivity. She needed Zachary back.

CHAPTER 12

Zachary hadn't told Ezaray how long he'd be. The rental car was traceable. He didn't want its final destination anywhere near Alder Ridge. Nor did he want to chance it being traced to Hull Creek. He drove to the next town east to drop it off at their rental depot. Walking through the town until he reached the edge, he veered off into the woods. He pulled a bag from his pocket and stripped, putting everything inside. Before he shifted, he called Asher to check in with them. They'd dropped off all the girls and were heading back, ditching their rentals in other towns. He dropped his phone in the bag and began to shift.

Bones popped and a warm ache spread. He knew the grey wind flowed out and around him. Landing on four enormous paws, Zachary picked up the bag in his jaw and ran toward Alder Ridge, cutting through nature that gave the shortest distance instead of following the highways.

He stopped outside Nathan's home near the lake. Pulling on his jeans, he knocked on the door. Shaye peeked out before letting the door swing open.

"Hey."

"Hi, Zachary. How are the girls?"

"Okay when I left them. I'm just getting back from returning the rental. I wanted to ask you something."

"Go ahead."

"I want to buy a home here. Or land to build one of my own. I want the privacy you all have and I want to settle near Smoke."

Shaye blinked as her lips spread into an indulgent smile, one that showed pride in its recipient. "I'll look at Diana's listings first thing tomorrow and start a search from there."

"Thanks." His gratitude was gruff.

"That's the second time today you've thanked me and the second time today you've surprised me. What's changed with you?"

"One of those girls is my mate."

"Us mates seem to have that effect on you guys." She nudged his arm and stepped back inside. Zachary grunted and stripped, putting the pants back in the bag before he ran around the town to Asher's. He wanted his bike back.

He waved at Gwen once he started his bike, who'd stepped outside at the sound. The vibrations coursing through him settled his soul. He had one more stop to make before he returned to Shaye's old house.

Tucking the new helmet in the top box, he sped off. The traffic was slow for this time of day. Scents of fall whipped around him. The idea of settling into a home before winter fell on them gave him a new determination. While they weren't likely to be found in Shaye's old home, he felt too exposed, too out of his element to keep his mate safe. And to keep Holly safe, if she ever showed up.

He needed to contact Garrett soon. He trusted the hawk to call him as soon as possible, but it had been a day already.

Zachary started this looking for Holly. Rest wouldn't come until she was home where he'd promised.

He pulled into the driveway and swung his leg off the bike. Deciding to check the door to see if they listened to him, he twisted the knob and met resistance. With relief, he pulled out the key and unlocked it. Ezaray and Maggie were sitting on the couch, terrified eyes locked on him as he walked through. Ezaray's relaxed, but Maggie still eyed him for a moment before looking away.

"You girls okay?"

"Yes. We've settled in. The clothes don't quite fit either of us, but they'll work fine for now. It's a nice house." Words poured from her with nervousness as Ezaray walked toward him, but stopped a few feet away. Uncertainty stiffened her stance. He closed the distance and ran his knuckle down her cheek.

"I'll get clothes that fit both of you in the next few days." He enjoyed her shiver as he continued from her cheek down her neck. "You two are free to come and go, but only with an escort for the first little while. Until we find out what we can about Tyrone and his organization."

"What about the rest of the girls?" The first words he'd ever heard from Maggie.

"We've told them the same thing. To lie low for at least a week. Watch the news for details on Tyrone."

Maggie nodded and went up the stairs. There was a lightness about her, but not a happy glow. She was quiet and airy as she moved. She should be in a place where she would get the help she needed after being a captive for so long. Not here with strangers.

Alone and free, he stood with a woman who didn't know who she was meant to be. So many urges came soaring to life.

"Ezaray, I need to do something and if you're not okay with it, you need to stop me." Zachary slid his hands around her waist and pulled her against him. With her curves matching his, his body turned into flames and his eyes sparked. He was thankful he didn't have to hide that part of him from her, but there was so much she needed to know.

"Zachary?"

He couldn't answer her. Leaning down, he stopped an inch from her lips. Her breath tickled his bottom lip. He waited until she leaned into him, trying to reach for the kiss he was promising. Zachary captured her lips with his. Coaxing and stroking with his tongue. She gasped, and he invaded. The taste of sweet cherries exploded. A growl escaped his chest, and it was more difficult than he expected not to devour her. He felt like the big bad wolf who'd caught little red. A dark-haired little red who he didn't want to scare away. Red Riding Hood never had red hair, anyway.

He deepened the kiss and pulled her until she stood on her tiptoes. Zachary freed her lips, but didn't let go of her body. Her breasts and hips nestled against his hardness. She was lean, but soft in the right places. He couldn't wait to see her beauty as she regained herself.

"Is this why you wanted me to come with you?"

"This and so much more."

She rushed to ask another question, but Zachary stopped her with another kiss. Just as deep as the first, he took his time and let his hands stroke her sides and down over her ass. Sweet cherries and arousal filled his senses. Damn it. He needed to stop before he took this to a place it shouldn't. "I'll explain it all soon, but not tonight. Not here."

"Okay." Her disappointment stung. With an encouraging twist around her waist, he turned her toward the stairs and gave her a nudge.

"Rest first." He followed her to the room she chose to make sure she settled in. She turned in the doorway, her eyes looking to the floor.

"Will you stay with me?"

"If that's what you want." He lifted her chin so he could see her answer in her eyes and not only hear it in her words.

"That's what I want."

"Okay." It would be agonizing pleasure to lie next to her, but not touch her the way he so desperately needed.

Ezaray took a pair of pajamas from the top drawer and disappeared into the bathroom. Zachary took one of the extra blankets from the top of the dresser and settled on top of the quilt on one side of the bed. He refused to tempt himself with getting too close before she was ready.

She came out and settled herself on her side, but didn't lie down and rest her head. She looked at him and her lips twisted. Words she wanted to let out, but too afraid to ask.

"What is it?"

"I want you to hold me." Her voice may have quaked, but she boldly told him what she needed.

"Anything you want." Never would he refuse her. He lifted his arm and with the blankets between them, she pushed herself against him and laid her head on his shoulder. He stroked her shoulder over her pajamas until her breathing evened.

With one goal accomplished, Zachary struggled with how to start a relationship with his mate.

EZARAY WOKE AGAINST SOMETHING HARD. Blinking rapidly, she froze and took in the room. The sweet bedroom of the house they were staying in came into focus. The hardness she lay against was Zachary.

"Good morning." His husky growl sent shivers over her body, but it was a warm shiver that reflected the kiss from the night before. He'd kissed her and touched, then she'd asked him to stay with her. It was all a bit much, but she didn't want to complain as she was just as attracted to him as it seemed he was to her.

Dampness coated her front. She hadn't moved the entire night; the blankets trapped between them. She pulled off him to allow her front to cool off. The sweat would soon dry.

"Good morning," she returned and looked up at him. His hair was out of place and he had one arm sprawled above him. He'd slept in his clothes from yesterday. Black t-shirt and jeans. "I'm sorry."

"For what?"

"Sleeping on you like that. I'm sweaty and I didn't even give you a chance to change your clothes."

"You have nothing to be sorry for." Zachary lifted the hand that held her all night and ran a finger through her hair. "I'm going to go shower. Don't get out of bed."

Ezaray nodded and laid back down to watch him leave the room. He came back a few minutes later with a fresh shirt and jeans in his hand.

"There are only two bathrooms in the house. Do you mind if we share one and let Maggie have her own?"

"Of course."

The bathroom door closed, and she heard the shower start. She wondered why he didn't leave her and Maggie here and go back to his own home. Why stay here with them? Did he believe Tyrone would find them? He wouldn't be staying here because of her. But deep down, she knew that was the case. She felt it too. Not knowing what it was, she couldn't explain it, but there was something there. She no longer had the experience to understand.

The water shut off, and he moved around in the bathroom. The water in the sink ran while he brushed his teeth. Zachary stepped out and Ezaray rolled over in bed. His hair was damp and fell over his forehead, looking blacker than the black it already was. He wore the same type of outfit as before, except now his t-shirt was a dark grey. The scent of clean soap wafted with the steam from the bathroom and surrounded him. He stood staring at her from the doorway. And she refused to move away from him despite her mind demanding they do.

"Are you okay?" he asked.

"I don't know what I am." That answer rang with more truth than what Ezaray was prepared for.

"It's only been a day. It'll take time." His mouth pinched closed. "I'll give you some privacy. I'll meet you downstairs." He took a step forward, but changed his direction toward the door.

Ezaray almost liked the idea of lying in bed. She had no reason to get up. No training that was being demanded of her. No fights, no meal she needed to have to ensure she stayed in perfect health. She wouldn't have to look over her shoulder in the kitchen to see if any of the other girls were scheming. Even if she didn't trust Maggie, she had Zachary here watching every part of her.

But lying in bed wasn't working. Her mind raced with the events of the escape and with what Tyrone would do now. Nope. She wouldn't put herself through that.

Throwing the covers off her, she walked to the bathroom to wash up, brush her teeth, and pull her hair back. Her hair reached below her waist now. Two years without a haircut left a heavy weight on her head. What had been bangs now framed her face and halfway down her neck. She normally kept her hair at shoulder length. Ezaray watched herself run the brush through the dark strands in the mirror with long strokes, enjoying the softness the feminine shampoo had given it. There'd been mirrors in the bathrooms and the training room with Tyrone, but she never thought to look at herself. There wouldn't have been anything she could have done to help her appearance if it had been a problem. She wouldn't have seen herself if she'd looked then. But looking now, it was like seeing an old friend, a face she recognized, but couldn't remember her name.

Ezaray shook her head and set down the brush. A mirror wouldn't help her right now.

She found another set of clothes that fit enough to wear for the day and went downstairs. Sizzling sounds from a frying pan and the smell of breakfast filled the house. Zachary stood at the stove in the kitchen and turned when she entered.

"Ready to eat?"

"Yes, please. I guess we didn't eat much on the road."

"I didn't want to take the time. Sorry about that."

"I'd rather starve for a few days than be back there." Ezaray mumbled, but he still heard her, judging by the quirk of his brow. He set down two plates at the table, but before he sat, Maggie walked in. Without a word, Zachary filled another plate and came back to the table.

Maggie eyed it, but didn't take her seat even though Zachary already had sand Ezaray had started eating. Time. This was all weird to both of them. With obvious caution, Maggie sat and picked at her food.

"Are you okay?" Ezaray tilted her head to catch Maggie's eye. She looked up and nodded. "Did you sleep well?" Again, Maggie nodded. She'd spoken to Ezaray when they were alone, but not in front of Zachary — except the once. And they hadn't heard her speak the entire two years under Tyrone, until she agreed to help them. Ezaray wanted to know so much about her.

Zachary sat with his empty plate in front of him while he waited for them to finish. Once they did, he piled the plates and took them all out. He had the kitchen cleaned before Ezaray thought about what she should do to help.

"What do we do now?" She was lost without the routine they'd had, and she assumed Maggie felt the same.

"Whatever it is you guys need."

"I don't think we know what that is."

"Let's start with Maggie." Zachary sat back down at the table and turned a sharp gaze on her. His body visibly relaxed, but it didn't matter what his mood, he was an intimidating figure. Maggie shrank back in her chair. Ezaray leaned forward to examine his face. Those eyes pinned Maggie in place, but nothing cruel emanated from him. Maggie needed to learn to trust him.

Just as Ezaray had.

ZACHARY KNEW what he wanted to do with Ezaray today. But he couldn't leave Maggie here alone without first attempting to talk to her.

"Where's home, Maggie? And why don't you want to go there?"

Large blue eyes shifted between him and Ezaray. Zachary was pushing, and he didn't care. His purpose had been to rescue Holly and Ezaray. He did that and rescued them all. But they weren't supposed to be his responsibility after that. He wasn't equipped to handle strange women, women who'd been through trauma.

"My only family is my step-brother. He's never been kind." Although quiet, her voice was clear.

"What about friends?"

"None." Her answer dropped with disdain. There was more behind that, but that wasn't something he needed to pry from her right now.

"Where are you from?"

"The city."

"Well, I understand why you didn't want to stay there." Ezaray reached across the small table and placed her hand over Maggie's.

"You need to decide where you want to go from here. You're welcome to stay for as long as you need, but you'll need to find a direction for yourself. I'll make sure you get whatever help you need."

"Thank you."

"Ezaray." He turned in his chair to face his mate. "I'd like to take you somewhere today if you want to go out."

"I think I'd like that."

"Maggie, I can send someone to take you out if that's what you'd like to do today or I can send someone to stay with you if you're more comfortable with that."

"I'm fine on my own."

Zachary nodded and stood, holding his hand out to Ezaray. He nodded at Maggie as they left. There was relief in his thoughts now that she'd spoken to him and given him some information about herself. At least now he understood why she came with them. He'd talk to Asher about what aid was out there for someone in her situation. Asher had enough connections with the right people in Alder Ridge to know the next step.

He took Ezaray outside, her hand still in his. They lost contact with each other when she froze and he kept walking.

"I'm not getting on that." She stared at his bike.

"Yes, you are." He wanted to go back to her and pull her closer, but he kept going toward his bike. Opening the top box, he pulled out the helmet and leather jacket he'd bought her. "Come here."

Her body shook, and she shook her head.

With patience he didn't know existed inside him, Zachary set her helmet and jacket on the seat and walked over to her. He framed her face and tilted her head back.

"I've got you." He hadn't intended to kiss her, but that's what he did. Leaning down, he captured her lips, soothing her trembles with his tongue. When he pulled up, he stepped back. Only when she took a step to follow did he let go of her face, regretting the loss of the smoothness beneath his rough fingertips.

He held up the jacket for her. She turned and slid her arms in. When she reached for the zipper, Zachary wrapped his arms around her from behind and zipped it for her. Any excuse he could get to touch her or hold her. His back curled around hers and he leaned his head down over her shoulder. Her quick breaths were tiny gasps as his hand slid further up her torso and his wrist brushed over her breast under the thick leather.

Gripping her shoulders, Zachary turned her around. The jacket fit perfectly, hugging her at her waist. He put the helmet on her head and went about adjusting the strap until it was snug and didn't wobble.

"Ready?"

"Not a bit," she said directly on the heels of his question.

"Hold on tight to me and move your body with mine.

Don't fight it." Zachary put his helmet on and held out his hand. Pulling in a deep breath, Ezaray rested her hand in his and allowed him to help her on. He gave her a few minutes to adjust until she settled comfortably against his back. Her thighs bracketed his and her arms were squeezing him tight. Never would he complain to have her this close.

He squeezed her hands and looked over his shoulder to nod, telling her he was going to move now. He tilted the bike up and started the engine. Using his feet, he backed out of the driveway.

A comical yelp came from behind him when he picked up speed outside of the neighbourhood. He took his time weaving through and around town, feeling pride in his little mate as she relaxed. Her instincts kicked in and she naturally followed his movements.

Zachary parked at Asher's. No one was home, and that was fine with him. He didn't bring her here to make introductions. Except to Smoke. Smoke came back before the escape, and Zachary needed to see him. And he needed to talk to Ezaray about what he was and learn about her.

He helped her with her helmet and jacket. The weather was mild enough the sweater she wore beneath it would be enough. He put his on the bike beside hers.

"Who lives here?"

"Asher. But we aren't here to see him."

"What are we here for?"

"To go for a hike." He nodded into the woods and hoped she wouldn't turn her nose up at the idea. But what he saw in her eyes stopped his heart. A moment of pure peace shimmered in the green. She'd been locked up in a concrete building for two years. She saw her freedom in front of her.

Zachary hoped she still felt free after he explained she was his mate.

CHAPTER 13

Ezaray tried to speed up when she noticed Zachary shortening his stride, but she wanted to take it all in. She'd taken this for granted before her captivity.

"Tell me about yourself, before they captured you."

"I'd been about to start a new job. I was twenty and enjoying life. Still trying to find myself." It all seemed so insignificant now. "I was sporty growing up. Played anything I had time for. But none of them carried over after high school. It was all for fun."

"Probably why you were such a good fighter."

"Yeah." She'd thought the same. "Whatever career path I was looking down doesn't matter anymore. I don't even know what interests I have. I'm not the same person I was two years ago."

"I don't imagine you are. Neither am I."

"What changed for you?" Ezaray looked up, eager to learn more about this man she couldn't turn away from.

"I've been on a mad search for Holly since the day she went missing."

"You've been searching non-stop for two years?" So much loyalty from a man so dark.

"For several months, I searched alone. When that didn't work, I traced back and found the trail from the beginning. I worked my way into an organization. One that takes women to sell or finds them when they already have a buyer. A few months ago, I got a tip with the address of the building. It was pure luck I got inside. The doctor helped me stay there."

"You upended your entire life to find her." Tears flooded behind her eyes with that kind of devotion. And for someone he hadn't seen in twelve years, someone he'd known as a child.

"Yeah, I did." He stopped walking and turned to her. His thumb swiped at her cheek. "Why the tears?"

"You love her that much."

"She's my baby sister." Ezaray understood. They weren't true siblings, but Holly talked of him with the same affection.

"How come you didn't keep in touch with her?"

"I became the idiot teenager everyone thought I already was. I regret every day that passed that I didn't talk to her." With each word, his voice got lower, growling and scolding himself. She wanted to comfort him, but he turned and started walking again. The only difference was now he held her hand.

She looked down at her hand engulfed by his, his darker skin hiding her pale tone, and wondered if he was that loyal to everyone he loved.

They rose over a grassy hill and down the other side before he paused.

"You know what I am. How much has Holly shared with you about being a shifter?"

"She's shown me her twin owl and shown me what she

looks like after she changes. They're identical. She has stronger senses, stamina, and strength. And I swear she never got sick with a cold, but she thinks that's luck."

"Not luck." Zachary shook his head. "Has she shown you what it looks like when she changes?"

"No." And Ezaray had never asked. Life hadn't been all that different. She just had a best friend that changed into an owl.

Zachary let go of her hand and stepped away. "Do you want to see?"

She nodded. She was about to come face to face with a wolf. Ezaray held onto Zachary's eyes. Those would always show his true self. But she lost her focus when he started pulling his shirt over his head. Her hands jumped to cover her eyes.

"What are you doing?"

Zachary chuckled, but Ezaray refused to look, no matter how much she wanted to see what he looked like when he laughed. She imagined the facial hair on his face changing shaped, the permanent scowl around his eyes crinkling and lifting. "I'm taking my clothes off."

"All of them?" Ezaray cringed as she squeaked.

"Yes, all of them."

"Why?" She pushed her hands harder against her face and turned her head.

"I can't shift with clothes on."

She listened to his footsteps over the grass and rustle in the bushes. Suddenly she felt a heated wall appear in front of her. Hard hands encased her wrists and pulled them away from her face.

"Open your eyes, little red."

"Little red?" She snapped her gaze to his face. "Why would you call me that?"

A wicked grin split his lips. He held her hands against his bare chest and she realized how trapped she was.

"You're the big bad wolf."

"You've got it, red." He bent down and kissed her. Nothing quick and nothing slow. He worked his lips over hers until she gave him the freedom to run his tongue over the seam. One hand released her wrist and ran up her arm. The heat trail started at her wrist, over her shoulder and down her back. Zachary pulled her against him and his erection settled hard against her belly. She flinched, and he paused, but he wasn't letting her go. He slowed the kiss until her muscles relaxed. Ezaray was aware of her position, his nakedness, her suddenly heavy clothes, and her inexperience. These past two years would have been full of so much learning and growth. But right now, she may as well still be twenty. Barely dipping her toes into this part of her life.

He lifted his head.

"You can't watch me shift with your eyes closed." Of course she couldn't.

Zachary stepped back in his glorified naked form and Ezaray kept her chin up, her eyes focused on his hair. Just his hair. Until she heard the first bone pop.

She gasped as more popped and moved out of place. It all looked painful until something about the transformation changed. What looked like smoke emerged from him and curled around him. Magic took over what the physical change couldn't.

Is this what it looked like for Holly? Such a smaller animal. It had to be more painful for her.

As the grey swirls dissipated, a dark grey wolf stood where Zachary had been only moments before. He was beautiful. A fiercely wild animal stared back at her, but just as she'd expected, she saw the man in his eyes. Those glowing lines of silver.

With slow steps, he advanced toward her. She had to repeat to herself that this was Zachary. It didn't matter what she knew at heart, there was still a wolf walking toward her. Prowling toward her. His little red reference was spot on. Red riding hood didn't have red hair, anyway.

Zachary didn't pause once he reached her. He pressed his nose to her stomach, then tilted his head to nudge against her. With more caution than she intended, Ezaray placed her hands on his head. His fur was soft beneath her fingers. She pushed them down over his neck.

"I'm speechless."

He ran his nose along her ribs and inhaled. Zachary turned and crouched down to the ground. Looking over his shoulder at her, he waited.

"What?"

Zachary swung his head toward his back.

"Seriously? You want me to ride you?"

A wolf lifting his brow was comical and she couldn't stop her giggle until she realized the double meaning of her words. Heat flared in her cheeks. Swallowing, she ignored what she'd said.

Climbing onto his back, she gripped his fur when he stood up. He didn't move until she had a firm grasp, then he started on a trot.

The ride was oddly calming. The cool air carried a scent she was no longer familiar with. As she watched the trees pass, Ezaray decided she never wanted to leave this place. It would be too easy to stay lost in the wilderness to live out the rest of her days.

Zachary picked up the pace and Ezaray let out a surprised squeal. She leaned down to wrap her arms around his neck and thought she could stay out here as long as Zachary stayed with her.

As Zachary ran through the woods with Ezaray on his back, he realized he hadn't processed the fact he'd found his mate. He'd told Asher and Nathan he had no intention of finding one or chasing after her. Finding her in danger never gave him the time to come to terms with how his life would change. But now, his thoughts naturally adjusted to include Ezaray.

The weather was cooler, but the air filled with a fresh crispness he'd missed while being in the city. He was ready to make the move to Alder Ridge permanent. He supposed it was time to consider what he'd do for work. Repairing motorcycles at his uncle's garage gave him what he needed. Creating his own business in Alder Ridge appealed to him now, when before, that ambition didn't exist. But he found since meeting Asher, his perspective on a lot of things had changed.

The small woman on his back became his world with shocking clarity. And as soon as he found Holly, he'd be at peace.

Zachary slowed as they approached the building, and he came to a stop as he sniffed the air. Wolves approached. Smoke and Kai appeared over the ridge. Ezaray's grip tightened and she lowered herself further on his back. He crouched to the ground, but she wouldn't let go. Motioning with his head, he pushed up with his legs like a hop to bounce her.

"They won't eat me?"

If a wolf could laugh, he would. Zachary shook his head

and waited for her to get off. He stepped out of her reach and shifted.

Her eyes locked onto him and followed the pattern of the wind.

"You know about Holly's owl. Every shifter that we know of has an animal pair. This is Smoke and Kai. Mine and Asher's pairs. Wolf brother is what I've always called him." He looked toward the wolves. "This is Ezaray." He left off the introduction as his mate.

Smoke wasn't shy. He walked over to her and stuck his head under her hand like he did to Gwen every time he saw her. Smoke saw her as family.

Ezaray stopped breathing, but she moved her hand over his head. Zachary walked toward the building.

"Don't you dare leave me." She lost the urgency in her calm monotone as if she were scared to spook the beast beneath her hand. Zachary chuckled.

"I'm not going far. It's just a little cold out here."

"Oh." She looked up. "Oh." Her cheeks turned rosy, and she looked away. He enjoyed her bashfulness. But her rapid blinking and short breath told him what he needed to know. Things weren't right in her world, but she was right with him.

He kept walking to the building and found a pair of jeans in the stash. Zachary returned to find Ezaray watching Smoke and Kai playing.

"They're amazing."

"They are. I'm in awe of them every day." That was a truth he didn't admit like he should.

"What did we come up here for?" Ezaray turned her head, but when she came eye level with his chest, her head shot up.

"Bored already?" He didn't feel at all bad about towering over her, letting a smirk play on his lips.

She smiled, a hint of something sweet and fun shining through for a brief moment.

"I wanted to show you the other side of me and to introduce you to Smoke. The privacy is nice too."

"I haven't had privacy in a long time."

"I don't imagine you have."

She took a deep breath that changed the subject on its own and stepped away from him. "What is this place?"

"A safe house or headquarters of some sort. Asher is building this for all the shifters we meet. A place they can hide when needed. A place to come for help."

"Sounds noble."

He grinned at her assessment. Noble described Asher perfectly. "That it is. Want a tour?"

"Sure." She followed him to the house. The heat of her eyes traced patterns on his back. It seemed as long as he wasn't watching her watch him, she didn't have a problem looking her fill. Zachary worried about the damage caused by what she'd been through. The attraction with the mate bond took over her senses, but would it be enough? Trauma could resurface later, but he believed it wouldn't cause difficulty. After seeing what Shaye and Nathan went through and the results of Asher's and Gwen's mating, he trusted that mates were meant to be and Fate wouldn't force them together unless they'd be happy. A month ago, he wouldn't have agreed with that. Now? He wasn't always happy with Fate, but she worked together with others to create what was right.

The house was coming along well. Walls, floor, and ceiling displayed the shell and left room to imagine the possibilities for the inside. Now that they finished the roof, they'd stashed some things for them to use. Some non-perishables in the kitchen and some things that could be cooked over a fire. Duffel bags of clothes of different types and sizes were in all the future bedrooms along with mattresses sitting on the floor with rolled up sleeping bags.

"Where did the wolves, Smoke and Kai, come from?"

"Their pack is nearby. Some things happened when Asher met Gwen, forcing Kai's pack deeper into the woods. But he loved the safety of it and told Asher he didn't want to move. So Asher built this place close to the pack. We're surrounded by nothing but free space for more packs or families to move in as needed. Nathan's bear created a den of his own up this way too."

"Did you name your wolf?"

"I did," he answered slowly.

"Why Smoke?"

"Did you see the grey wind when I shifted?"

"Yes."

"When I first shifted, I thought the wind was smoke. It swirled around myself and the wolf pup. It was the first name that came to mind for the brother I'd been paired with."

Ezaray walked the living space on her own, circling as she looked around. "This house is amazing. I love how secluded it is."

"Now that you're free, where do you want to live?" It wasn't a fair question. She'd only been free for a day, and he hadn't given her a chance to return home. But he wanted to know where she longed to be. "Have you had a dream of a home?"

They strolled back outside to watch the wolves playing. More from the pack had joined them, both alphas teaching the others. The wind chilled his bare skin, but the last thing he would do in front of Ezaray was complain. There were shirts in the bags in the bedrooms, but not the quick grab one near the front of the building where he'd grabbed the jeans.

"Two years ago, I wouldn't have had a clue. Or maybe I would, but it wouldn't have been something I'd have stuck with. Now, it's different. All of this appeals to me right now."

But time could change her mind.

"Zachary?" She looked up at him. Her eyes carried their own confusion. "Is there something going on that I'm not seeing?"

"Yeah, little red. There is." He couldn't lie to her. But neither was she ready for the truth. He let her feelings reign and take over, pushing his down. He wouldn't allow his instincts to overrun her needs.

Zachary pulled her against him, happy she leaned with him and her hands landed on his chest. Although, she hesitated and lifted them away. A quick breath and she pushed her palms back against his skin and spread her fingers. The warmth from her shocked him. His cock strained against the already tight jeans.

He might not be willing to tell her she was his mate, but he wasn't against showing her and seeing what she did with the information.

Brushing his lips against hers, once, twice. He gave her the opportunity to pull away, even though she hadn't before. Zachary kissed her, seducing her lips over and over. Licking, kissing, moving, sucking.

When she let her hands free, moving up with her sigh that escaped her lungs, Zachary moved his hands from her waist down to her ass. Round and small, the globes fit in his palms. He lifted her against him. Her lips parted as she gasped at the extra contact of his cock against her stomach.

A single cold drop landed on his shoulder. He hadn't checked the weather before leaving. But neither did he care. He'd stand in whatever weather came their way as long as he had her in his arms.

🐺

RAIN BEGAN DROP BY DROP, but Zachary never changed his motions or grasp. Ezaray wondered what she should do. But it didn't matter what she tried to tell herself, pull back and run to shelter, keep a hold on him, or stop everything, she didn't listen to herself. She allowed Zachary's body to control her. Her instincts fed off of his.

Maybe this was all too soon, but could she say she didn't trust him? No. She trusted him with her entire being. Him and his friends. They'd done the unbelievable and rescued them. All of them. It wasn't only her that was free. Her friends and even the girls she didn't like. She wouldn't judge a single one of them for their behaviour. She may not have liked some of them, but none of them deserved to be in there. Who knew what she would have been like in there if she hadn't had Holly by her side.

This man wasn't just her hero. There was something else she didn't understand. He admitted it himself. And that was when he grabbed and kissed her. This was what she wasn't seeing, but that made little sense. Words weren't his explanation. Instincts were.

The rain rushed down around them, droplets streamed down his skin and drenched her shirt. But there they stood.

"Zachary, please?" The plea against his lips came from nowhere. She didn't know what she wanted or why.

"I'm here, little red." And one of his hands moved.

It skated with a slick motion around her hip and to the

button on her fly. The jeans she wore were now soaked. They would be agony to get off when they got back. They were already too tight.

None of that stopped Zachary. She froze, waiting to feel anything he could give her as he undid the button and zipper and slid his large hand beneath. He didn't seem fazed about the lack of room. He pushed his hand in far enough to position his fingers in the right place.

The rain hitting her body in heavy drops matched the rhythm of his finger pulsing against her clit. Thank God she wasn't a virgin, but she wasn't ready for a man like Zachary.

Soon her breathing picked up tempo, and he brought unbearable pleasure from a single finger.

Her mind crashed back to the surface, and she pulled away. She looked up and winced under the onslaught of the water. Zachary didn't follow her or pull her back. He didn't tighten his grip. Ezaray had whatever control she wanted to have. She hadn't had control of her life for two years. What would she choose now that she had the choice?

She wouldn't choose anything that didn't involve Zachary.

Ezaray looked back at him, his hair stuck to his forehead and lines of water ran down his face. His chest heaved beneath her hands — the bare skin hot to the touch.

"Show me what I'm missing."

His eyes widened and each of his fingertips increased their pressure against her body. The muscles along his jaw ticked.

"You're not ready, Ezaray."

"I don't care. Show me."

With a growl, he pulled his hand free and lifted her, her wet clothes sticking to his skin. He walked toward the building and carried her inside through the doorway that didn't have a door. Wet footprints trailed behind him as he walked through to one of the bedrooms. Each room was enormous, so the small double mattress that lay on the floor looked too small to house a normal sized human, let alone a large wolf shifter.

He set her on her feet.

"Ezaray, you have the control here. You asked me to show you and I don't think you're ready, but I can't deny you anything. Tell me to stop. Now." He demanded her to refuse him.

"No." She wouldn't refuse herself something she knew would be wonderful. Why would she? She spent two years in a form of hell. She wouldn't deny herself anything good in life.

"Ezaray." His husky voice growled, and she was sure he meant it to be a warning, but that wasn't what she heard. The sound and the vibrations scored through her.

"Show me. Please." She'd never begged in captivity. But to Zachary, she'd beg.

"Fuck." He cursed, but his hands gripped the hem of her sweater and pulled it up.

Zachary didn't touch her skin after removing her shirt. He went to work on the clasp of the bra and in seconds it loosened around her chest and he pulled it down her arms. It took him some effort, but he peeled her jeans over her hips.

He bent down on one knee and peeled them off of each leg. His calluses rough against her cold skin sent shivers up her legs. When she stepped free of the denim, Zachary didn't stand. He looked up at her and her shivers raced over her entire body.

With her eyes trapped in his, he pulled her panties down. She couldn't move. Slow and steady movements, he stood and clasped his hands around her waist, walking her back toward the bare mattress.

"Lay down." His words darkened with his command. Ezaray lowered herself to the mattress and sank back into the softness. Zachary's hand went to his fly, and he released his cock when he pushed the jeans down. The soft slapping sound of them hitting the floor was loud in the room. Her eyes stretched over his body. She expected a man as dark as him to have tattoos, but nothing marred his tanned skin. Not a single muscle relaxed. They twitched and pulsed in a rhythm she recognized in her own body.

Her eyes met his, flashing bright.

"Have you seen enough?" He smirked, but his impatience was clear.

"Never," she whispered, surprised at her own courage.

Letting out a rough sound from his gut, he lowered himself to the mattress, tracing his hand up her leg as he covered her. "Is there anything I need to know?"

She had to let the fog clear from her mind to figure out what he was asking. "No."

He squeezed her hip and captured her lips. The fog settled over her mind again and she was happy to lose herself in the mist.

CHAPTER 14

Terrified, Zachary worried he'd do something wrong. But he smelled her arousal. Her emotions were where they should be in a moment like this. He lowered his body to hers. Their skin, still wet from the rain, was quickly drying from their heat.

He kept their lips sealed while his hand explored, venturing up and down her side, over her hips and down her thigh. Sliding it over her stomach, he let his fingers skim above her clit. Zachary wanted to taste the goosebumps trailing under his hand on her perfect skin. He lifted and looked down at her, needing to check in with her once more.

"You ready, little red?"

Her lips twitched, and she nodded.

Zachary watched her face change as he moved his hand between her legs. He brushed over her lips and lower, gathering her arousal on his fingers. Ezaray gasped when he placed a single finger over her clit. Her legs spread willingly, allowing him better access.

It was a struggle to move slow, but rushing wasn't an

option. Her nipples tightened and begged him for attention. Bending his head, he captured and sucked, matching the rhythm of his finger. As soon as her hips bucked once, Zachary slid his hand lower and plunged a finger into her heat. She cried out in pleasure and her hands held his head tight against her breast, her fingers tangling in his hair.

With that reaction, Zachary no longer needed to worry about her.

He dragged his finger in and out of her before adding a second. The fit was snug and his cock jumped, impatiently waiting for its turn.

Zachary nipped at the nub in his mouth, working it between his teeth.

The rain thundered against the roof, but it wasn't loud enough to drown Ezaray's cries and moans. This wasn't even the start of the things he could do to her, the places he could take her. He lifted his head, her hands still pulling on his hair.

"I can't wait to feel you come around my fingers." He curled his fingers to hit her sweet spot, following her as her hips bucked and she tried to retreat from the intense sensation. He placed his thumb over the hood of her clit and worked her core until he felt the first tremors. "Come for me, Ezaray. So I can fuck you like we both need."

Ezaray gasped and her eyes locked on his. He watched them roll back before her lids closed at the same moment her walls clamped down on his fingers. Zachary didn't stop his motions, wringing every single pulse from her body and listening to every moan from her lips.

His.

She didn't know, and he hadn't claimed her, but deep inside, the truth settled and made a home. *Mate* screamed through his mind.

Once her eyes opened and looked back up at him, he dragged his hand free and brought his fingers to his lips. He put them in his mouth and sucked them clean. Her cheeks flamed.

"Sweet cherries. You taste just as I've imagined."

"How long have you been imagining that?" she rasped.

"Since the second I met you."

He kissed her, pushing his tongue in to give her her own flavour. With one knee, he wedged her legs further apart then settled himself between. His cock bumped against her centre, the tip moving through her wetness.

Taking himself in hand, he used slow, short thrusts to work his way in. Ezaray stopped breathing, but Zachary didn't pause. Several long, agonizing minutes later, he seated fully inside her. He stayed there, his own breathing laboured, and Ezaray drew a long breath.

"You with me, little red?" he growled against her cheek.

"Uh huh."

Instincts took over, and he set a steady, forceful rhythm. A growl rumbled as his fangs lengthened. The urge to mark her came soaring forth. Zachary hadn't believed Asher and Nathan when they told him how strong the desire to bite her would be. He pulled his face further from her neck and touched his forehead to hers. Grinding his teeth, he focused on bringing her to her peak. He wouldn't finish. Not this time.

Pin pricks of pain created a line on each shoulder. Ezaray's grip tightened with each thrust. He ground his pelvis against hers to bring her closer. The closer she got, the closer he was. It was a race he had to lose.

She cried out in between gasps as her walls squeezed his cock. He had to get out before he lost control, filling and marking her. Just a little longer. He rode through her spasms until she relaxed against the mattress.

Ripping himself from her, he held himself up with straight arms. Quivers racked him, trying to loosen his tension and give him release.

When he opened his eyes, she was staring up at him, confusion filling her features. Fuck, he'd hurt her.

"You didn't..."

"Not this time, lovely."

"Oh."

He cupped her face. "It's not because I don't want to. I don't want to risk losing control." He didn't have the control to stop himself from biting her, marking her as his mate. It was irreversible and she didn't yet know what it meant.

"Of what?"

"A conversation for next time." Zachary stretched out beside her and pulled her against him.

"Will you do the same next time?"

"I fucking hope not." He felt her confusion, but it was still too soon to explain. Instead, he held his mate and listened to the rain while he planned how he would explain it all.

EZARAY TRIED NOT to feel hurt that Zachary had pulled out and then denied himself relief. Feeling both used and like she wasn't enough took away the euphoric pleasure she should still be in. It made little sense with how he'd been treating her.

Comfort and warmth surrounded her despite the chill racing over her bare skin. His arms wrapped around her and his fingers traced patterns on her arm. A motion that would normally tickle left rivers of heat. It warred with the rejection.

"Ezaray. I can feel you aren't happy. What's wrong?" His low tone broke through the sound of the rain.

"You can *feel* that?" She tilted her head back. His brows drew down.

"How much did Holly tell you? Shifters can sense emotions."

She chuckled. "That's how she always knew when I was lying."

"What's wrong?" Utter seriousness radiated from him. If he could sense emotions, then he'd be able to tell if she lied.

"I'm confused. What just happened, or what didn't happen, it doesn't match how you've been treating me. And none of that answered my question."

"What question?"

"What is it I'm not seeing?" She rolled over to rest her chin on her hand so she could see him, see his eyes when he answered her.

"I want to give you time. Maybe this never should have happened so soon, but it did. I'll hold back everything I can until you're ready."

"You're right." She didn't like that he was right.

"I'm sorry I hurt you."

"You didn't. I was just confused." But as he lifted his brow, she knew he sensed the lie. Ezaray laid her cheek against his chest.

"Doesn't sound like that rain is going to stop soon."

"It sounds beautiful though." Ezaray didn't want it to stop.

"Rest if you want, even sleep. I'm going to get some work done." He patted her hip. She looked back up at him.

"Work?"

"Give Asher some help and put some work into this place."

"I want to help." Her own excitement surprised her. She pushed up from his chest and stared at him, asking for permission to do something she didn't know how.

"Sure." His eyes slimmed as indulgence lifted his mouth with a grin. "Our clothes are still wet. I'll check all the bags to see if Gwen has left any of her clothes up here."

Ezaray didn't know who Gwen was, but she huddled on the mattress and watched his naked ass rummage first through the bag of clothes left in this room, then out the door to check the other bags. He came back dressed in a dry pair of jeans and carrying sweatpants and a large t-shirt.

"These should fit." He helped her stand and eyed her while she dressed. "I saw some materials ready in the kitchen. Let's work in there."

Zachary grabbed a tool belt from a pile of them near the front of the house. Rain had poured in through the vacant front door. This place was barely a shelter at this point.

"Will this be finished by winter?" Winter could hit early up this way, and the air had been chilly today.

"It has to be." He opened a box, revealing panels of wood, and looked at each one. Pulling out the first four, he nodded to the side. "Can you grab that bag of screws?"

A clear plastic bag with the top rolled open sat on the floor in front of her. Ezaray picked it up, and she followed him over to a wall with markings on it. "Are we putting together the cabinets?"

"We'll start them, yes."

She passed him screws and helped hold pieces together when needed. They started working on the next section and Zachary paused. He held out the drill to her.

"Here."

"I don't... I've never... nope." She stumbled over her embarrassing confession. Mischief filled his smile.

"Then it's time you learn."

Ezaray took the drill, surprised by its weight. For the next section, Zachary was the one passing her screws and holding pieces in place. It took longer. Her hesitancy created mistakes. He crouched behind her for the first few and helped use his force around her arms and hands.

It must have been hours that passed, but eventually they each had their own drill and worked at opposite ends. Zachary had twice as much work done, but Ezaray felt proud of the little work she did, trying hard to keep it straight. This wasn't her house. She didn't want to be at fault for screwing something up.

Zachary came over and leaned against the single section she finished on her own.

"You're a natural."

"Or I just had an excellent teacher."

"Maybe a bit of both." His one-sided smirk sent a flutter to her core. She'd slept with this man and she knew she wanted to do it again.

The room was silent long enough she realized the rain had stopped.

"We should get going. Maggie has been alone for a while." He said they should go, but he didn't move. If he wouldn't move, then neither would she. Ezaray waited while something stretched between them, reaching for the other. She couldn't be the only one that felt it.

Zachary took a step and wrapped his hands around her waist, his fingers splaying on her back and his thumbs drawing circles on her abdomen.

"If I kiss you again, we might not make it back. Make sure you push me away after a few minutes."

She giggled thinking he was joking, but his face stayed serious as he bent and kissed her with just as much heat as they'd felt in the rain.

⁌

SHE'D DONE as he'd asked. Ezaray had pushed him away, but with weak arms he hadn't gone far. However, the lack of contact sobered him enough he'd got them out the door. Ezaray had a better grip on his fur this time, so he'd raced through the woods, enjoying her laughter.

They'd arrived back at Shaye's to Maggie, who'd looked relaxed on the couch, but Zachary smelled panic on her skin. It receded the longer they'd been there. A tinge of guilt simmered. He shouldn't have left her here alone, but he'd been desperate for time alone with Ezaray. Zachary would give her a couple more days before speaking with her again about going home, or finding a home of her own.

Zachary considered making them dinner, but did takeout instead, thinking it had been a long time since they had something like that. He got them settled and left to pick up burgers, Chinese, and pizza, giving them choices and leftovers.

When he came back in, their heads lifted and their eyes widened. He hid his grin when he turned toward the kitchen.

Setting his phone on the table, watching it, he helped the girls dig in and he took whatever they didn't want of the burgers.

His attention turned to his phone too often. He needed to call Garrett. Just as the itching in his fingers was unbearable and he reached for his phone, it rang. He scraped the chair across the floor in his haste to stand up, answering and pulling his phone to his ear at the same time.

"Where is she?" he barked into the speaker.

"I've been on her tail since she reached the roof. She's been trying to lose me since and she did. I'm sorry. I'm still trying to find her. But she's safe. She hasn't shifted back. She's flying through the trees as an owl."

"Thanks for the update." Zachary wanted to yell. He wanted to demand more of the doctor, force him to find her and bring her home. But Zachary would have lost her trail much sooner.

"She'll come around when she's ready." Garret sounded like the doctor he was.

"Anything on Tyrone." Zachary had left the kitchen, but he still lowered his voice so the girls wouldn't overhear him.

"I got a call from him first thing this morning. I'm being watched and I'm suspended until further notice, with a distinct reminder of the consequences for going against him." The consequences being both Garrett's life and his sister's.

"Be careful."

"I'm fine, for now. I'll need to show up to some normal places soon. My disappearance will determine my guilt."

"As much as I want you to find Holly, go back to your life for a while. It's too dangerous if he suspects you. But call if you need help or he gets too close."

"Got it. Oh, and Zachary?"

"Yeah?"

"I told Holly how to find that building near the wolf pack. That's where she'll go if she goes to Alder Ridge on her own."

"Thanks Garrett."

"I'll come as soon as I can."

They ended the call and Zachary shoved his phone in his pocket before he broke it out of frustration. He took a step back toward the kitchen, but froze as the girls' voices filtered toward him. He wasn't enough of a gentleman to not listen in.

"How long are we staying here?"

"I don't know."

"I feel just as trapped being told to stay inside this house. Where did you go today?"

"He took me hiking. Maggie, you're allowed to leave. Zachary just said it's safer to have someone with you. He won't force you to stay here. He'll help you get to wherever you want to go safely."

"I don't even have a life to go back to. I don't know where I want to go."

"Why not start your life then?"

"But." Zachary heard her pull in a breath and hold it before her voice came out softer than before. "Never mind."

"Maggie," Ezaray started, but Zachary walked in and cut off their conversation. Maggie wouldn't say anything she didn't want to.

They both lifted their heads. Guilt shaded Maggie's blue eyes, turning the colour pale. Ezaray only sighed and started cleaning the table.

"Ezaray's right, Maggie." He stood across the table and held her guilty gaze until she stood and left the room on soft feet. He helped Ezaray with the cleanup. "Do you know of any reason she should feel guilty?"

"Guilty? No."

"Okay." He put the last of the containers in the fridge. "I want to spend as much time up at the building as possible. That's where Holly will go if she comes here."

"Who was on the phone?" Ezaray wiped her hands on a towel.

"Garrett." He wrapped his arms around her. "I want to go back there for the night, but I don't want to leave you here."

"I can come."

"Someone needs to stay with Maggie. She was scared before we came home."

"She was?" Her face softened. "Those are some helpful shifter senses."

"I can have someone come stay here, but I don't think she'll be comfortable with anyone but you."

"You're right." She turned her head down in disappointment. Her hands rested on his chest and she leaned her cheek against them.

"I can still have someone come stay with the both of you. You're not comfortable being alone either."

Ezaray shook her head with quick motions. Her fingers tightened on his shirt. It seemed she only wanted him.

"Are you sure?" He leaned his head down and placed a kiss on her hair.

"I'm sure. I'll try to talk to Maggie again tonight."

She looked up at him and although he wanted to leave, he couldn't let go of her. He tilted his head, knowing his size always intimidated, but not with Ezaray. The air thickened between them. Her tongue darted out to wet her lips and her eyes searched his.

Inwardly, he scolded himself. He wouldn't take her again today, but he could play with her.

Zachary moved his hands to her ass and lifted. She squeaked.

"Hush now," he chided. "Maggie's upstairs."

He carried her to the living room and laid her down on the couch, following her down.

"I don't think I can leave without making you come first."

Her shock only aroused him further. Ezaray looked over the arm of the couch toward the stairs, then back at him.

"Better be quiet, little red," he warned, feeling very much like the dangerous wolf.

Zachary let his fingers skim under the hem of her shirt and along the waist of her pants, thankful she'd changed into leggings when they got back from the woods. He flattened his hand against her stomach, feeling it cave in with her breath.

Pushing his hand up under her shirt, he pulled the cup of her bra down to reveal her breast. He filled his hand, her nipple rigid against his palm. Bending his head and sliding his hand to the side, he nipped her nipple through her shirt.

Ezaray gasped.

He nipped again and placed a finger over her lips to silence her as he drew her nipple into his mouth, her shirt becoming a damp barrier. His hand moved to her other breast and freed it from the cup. Lifting his head, he let her see his wicked grin.

Gently covering her mouth with his hand, holding in the sounds he knew she'd make, he bent his head to nip and suckle her other nipple. His other hand eagerly traced back down her stomach and disappeared in the waist of her leggings.

He craved to feel her bare skin against his, but if he removed any clothing, he'd fuck her on this couch. All he needed was her scent, her taste, to carry with him, to drive him insane through the night alone in the woods.

CHAPTER 15

Zachary's hand covered her mouth, sealing her lips. Ezaray whimpered, but that only made his grin around her nipple grow. The strong pulls of his mouth shot pleasure to her core. Pleasure that pulsed and jumped as his fingers played through her folds, spreading moisture.

Two fingers circled her entrance. Her pants keeping his hand snug against her. His eyes met hers with intensity as he plunged his fingers in.

She moaned against his hand, and he tightened his hold over her mouth.

Zachary had trapped her with his hands, his eyes, with pleasure, but never had she felt freer than she did under him.

His fingers curled, and his thumb found her clit. He lifted his head and stared down at her with steel eyes.

"Can I move my hand?"

She widened her eyes and shook her head as vigorous as she could under his grip. She didn't want to lose that contact, that control.

"You like it where it is." Satisfaction flared on his face and his chest rumbled like the low roll of thunder in the distance. "Come, Ezaray. Now. Before I lose it and fuck you instead."

His lips mirrored the lift of hers under his hand.

"Don't push me, little red. Not yet." She didn't ignore his plea, despite the excitement she saw cross his face. His fingers worked harder at her sweet spot and his thumb applied more pressure. She wouldn't be able to deny him, anyway.

Ezaray let go, pulling in all he gave her. It peaked and crested the edge. Her back arched as she climaxed in his hand. The hand on her mouth followed her movements as her back and neck bowed.

Even as her walls ceased squeezing him, Zachary still didn't remove either of his hands.

"I want to do so much more." His voice was hoarse as he slowly removed his hand from her mouth, but his fingers still played with light strokes.

Ezaray couldn't find her voice to agree with him.

He kissed her while his hands righted her clothes, taking advantage to tweak and play while he did. Zachary lifted off her and helped her up.

"Are you sure you'll be okay here tonight?"

She nodded.

"No words for me?" he teased. Ezaray cleared her throat.

"Aren't you a little old to be fooling around with a girl on the couch?"

Zachary laughed. It started as a chuckle and grew until his shoulders shook and his eyes glowed. "My, what a sharp tongue you have."

Ezaray's giggle was higher pitched than she'd have liked as he continued to play the part of the big bad wolf. But she'd be lying if she didn't love her role as Red Riding Hood.

Zachary kissed her, slow this time, before he left to watch for Holly. Ezaray took some time to rest on the couch, not ready to let go of all he gave her. But she took a steadying breath and stood.

Ezaray decided to push Maggie further. She went upstairs and gently tapped on her door. It took Maggie some time, but she opened the door a crack.

"Can we talk some more?"

"I guess so." Maggie let her in. She positioned herself on her bed in the centre and in a self-protected ball. Ezaray sat toward the end and pulled her feet up beside her.

"I don't know what to do or where to go either." Maybe if Ezaray opened up, it would be easier for Maggie. "My situation is different. I have a family to go home to, but I'm not ready to see them. The life I had planned before all this is obsolete. It doesn't matter, and it doesn't apply to who I am anymore. There's nothing around me that makes sense. Are we all expected to pick up where we left off? What's an acceptable time frame to heal after what we've been through?"

Maggie's features softened. Ezaray was getting through to her. Her walls were lowering.

"Maggie, are you afraid to be alone?"

"It's ridiculous. Alone is how I should feel safe. I've always just wanted to be left alone." Maggie looked away.

"It's not ridiculous. Why should there be rules to how we're feeling?" Saying it to Maggie also helped herself.

"Thank you for that."

"What about staying in Alder Ridge? Or is there another place you've always wanted to live?"

"Like I said, the only thing I ever wanted was to be left alone."

"Now you can. I'm still here. And we won't leave you

alone if you don't want. But now, whatever your previous life was, it's gone, if you want it to be. You're alone and free." She had the freedom to start over. They all did.

"I want a job. And I want to go learn something." Maggie's knees lowered and her spine straightened. Ezaray watched as a new dream formed inside her. "What do you want?"

Ezaray started this conversation intending to bare her feelings to help Maggie, but she didn't expect it to get turned around on her. "I don't know. Right now is hour by hour. I shouldn't be holding onto Zachary with such dependence, but I can't seem to help myself. I'm not ready to face my family. I will, but I can't do that without Holly. We should go home together."

"Where did she go?"

"I don't know that either." That wasn't an entire lie. "She ran with her freedom, I guess." More like flew with it. "Zachary is determined to find her."

"He came there looking for her, didn't he?"

"Yeah."

"But then he still saved all of us."

"Yeah." She had no words and Maggie was in just as much awe of the selfless act as she was.

ZACHARY WALKED into the house mid-morning. The girls had already eaten and had the kitchen cleaned. They sat on the couch, each with a book in their hand. Maggie glanced at him and gave a tiny nod, but went straight back to her book. Ezaray looked at him with eyes that begged for answers.

"Hey," she said.

"Hi." Zachary gave a small shake of his head to tell her there was no sign of Holly last night. In the kitchen, he made himself something to eat, not that he needed much. He'd hunted with Smoke last night and again this morning.

Feeling useless, he called Garrett while he ate his scrambled eggs.

"Hello."

"Hey. How are things going?"

"A lot of eyes. Look, I'm going to check in with you twice a day. If you don't hear from me for either of those, then Tyrone either found me out or jumped to a conclusion."

"Then why don't you disappear? Get away from it all."

"Once he lets up on me, I'm tracking him. I need to find out if he still has my sister. If by some miracle she's alive, and I disappear, Tyrone will kill her." Garrett didn't sound like he had much hope, but Zachary understood. He wouldn't have stopped until he found Holly, dead or alive. He hadn't stopped until he found her.

"I get it. But consider tracking him first, then disappearing."

"I'll think about it. You shouldn't come try to find me either. It will put all the girls at risk if you're discovered too, and he recognizes you from the club."

"Okay." Zachary didn't like leaving Garrett behind, but the hawk was right about the girls. He hung up the phone and checked in with Asher and Nathan. He hadn't spoken to them since they all got back.

Ezaray entered the kitchen on soft feet as he was ending the last call. Zachary pulled her onto his lap, setting a firm hand on her hip.

"Were you okay last night?"

"Yeah. We talked." She kept her hands in her lap, but still tilted her shoulders toward him. It spoke of shyness, as if she were still uncertain, maybe not understanding her feelings toward him.

Zachary raised his brow, curious about what Maggie had to say.

"Everything is fine. She'll be fine."

"She still doesn't want to go home or go somewhere to get help to get back on her feet?"

"Not yet, and never home. I didn't ask her to tell me about it."

Zachary pushed his frustration aside. He should focus on Ezaray's past, anyway.

He slid his hand over her cheek and pulled her down. Kissing her, he pulled in her scent and taste. He spent most of his time the night before as a wolf when he would have rather been cuddling up in the building with his mate. But Zachary didn't regret the time spent with Smoke.

Releasing her, she sat back.

"What job were you about to take before they took you?"

Ezaray scoffed and rolled her eyes. "It was a secretary position. I thought that was the best damn thing in the world. I'm not sure what I'll do now. I don't think I could ever have a job that I would have to be under that kind of authority."

"That's understandable. I've never been great with authority."

"You? No." She dragged out her words with mock surprise and disbelief, then her face lifted with a smile. He longed to see those on her.

"How would you know, little red?"

"I've only known you a very short time, but you radiate with an authority of your own. It also helps that I've heard all kinds of stories about you from Holly." So many times he'd get in trouble, and not every adventure had been his idea.

"I'd like to go have a nap."

"You didn't sleep at all, did you?" Concern filled her eyes.

"No, but it's not just a nap I need." Ezaray's lips fell apart as he saw understanding in her eyes. It wouldn't be long and he'd have to tell her what she was.

Zachary stood and let her slide off his lap. He turned her around and nudged her back to get her moving. His cock strained at his jeans and his blood hummed through his veins while a chant of *mate* sang in his ears.

They passed Maggie, who barely looked up from her book. Ezaray led them to the room she was staying in.

"I know what I need. I want to know what you need, little red."

The wonder that shone through her eyes and her long, shaky breaths built the moment higher. He wanted to hear her answer, what she desired of him.

She met his eyes, and he took a single step toward her.

"I want to feel so much. But not used."

"Never would I use you." Zachary closed the space between them, fast. One arm around her back pressed her body against his and his other hand clasped her jaw. "Never." He forced her face upward to see the sincerity in his eyes. His anger flashed at the thought.

"I want to feel special."

"Oh, little red. You are."

Zachary covered her mouth, quickly taking advantage to run his tongue along hers. He'd never get enough of her taste. When he lifted his head, he started stripping her of her clothes.

"Why don't you take what you want?" Her shirt fell to the floor, and he worked on her pants, pulling them down over her hips. He needed to get them out to shop for clothes of their own.

"I couldn't do that." Her nervousness was unexpected. His strong mate didn't want to take control. A devilish grin lifted his lips.

"Yes, you can." Zachary stepped back and took off his clothes, sending them to the same pile as hers. "I'll make sure you can."

He wrapped his hands around her ass and lifted to throw her on the bed. Ezaray squealed.

"Shhh. We still aren't alone." She clasped both of her hands over her mouth with mortification. Zachary grasped her knees and gave her a sinful look before he lowered his mouth to her core, eager to make her want it all.

EZARAY WASN'T DIRECTING any of this, but she wasn't about to complain and the last thing she would do is stop him. He threw her a purely sinful smile before his face disappeared. It showed a dark, playful side that she was beginning to love.

Her head tilted back as he drove her wild with his tongue, teeth, and lips. He used each part of his mouth in a calculating way. And when he added his fingers, her walls squeezed and quivered, ready to let loose an orgasm stronger than ever before.

She held her breath, muscles tense, ready and waiting. Pleasure stretched with long fingers. Everything collided together. Until suddenly she was empty.

Ezaray tore her head from the bed and glared at Zachary who now stood with his arms crossed and he had the grin of a satisfied cat who got the cream. That wasn't right. He was a wolf who'd won his fight for alpha. Dark and playful.

"What are you going to do? Does the wolf get you or do you get the wolf?" His sexy smirk and his rough tone worked in unison to send a delightful shiver down her spine.

Her clit throbbed and her core clenched. Ezaray fisted the sheets while his lips continued to taunt her. Something bubbled up inside her. Something she hadn't felt in a long time. A confidence she hadn't known she had back then. What was that saying? You don't know what you have until it's gone.

It was back now.

The pleasure pushing at the peak with urgency for release mixed with his arrogant challenge.

"I get the wolf."

"That's my girl." Zachary gripped her ankles and pulled her to the end of the bed. She sat up to take him in hand, but he lifted her in the air. Instinct wrapped her legs around him. When he sat down on the bed, Ezaray was in the perfect position. He leaned back, bracing himself on his hands. "Have at it, little red."

Ezaray hesitated for only a moment, not knowing how to begin, but it didn't last as she pulsed at the touch of his cock against her.

She lifted her hips enough to give her access, and she reached between them. Adjusting him so the tip met her entrance, she gasped. His muscles tensed beneath her other hand on his chest. Ezaray lowered herself. Curious to watch, she looked down until she couldn't see his cock at all. Then she looked into his eyes. They glowed bright, with a surreal, smoky swirl. His emotions always shone at the surface with her. If he allowed his eyes to glow like that all the time, he'd be discovered for what he is.

Ezaray slowly lifted herself, gasping as she dragged herself over him. Her movements were slow, but not for long. Still so close to her climax, her body took over for her and soon she undulated on him with intense urgency.

Zachary didn't move, but with her hands bracing on his chest, she felt his muscles ripple. His thighs tightened under her ass. Seeing his jaw lock, she knew he would try to hold off again.

"Please, don't," she begged, saddened by the loss of something that hadn't happened yet.

"Don't what?" he growled.

"Don't hold back."

"Ezaray, I have to."

"Why?" She didn't stop. In fact, she worked harder, trying to make him lose control with her.

"I'll do more than what you're ready for if I come with you."

Ezaray remembered he'd put her in control of this. If he wanted it that way, she would take control.

She threw her head back and selfishly took her pleasure. Her body went tense and her thighs squeezed his hips. Her walls contracted and pleasure shot out from her core to fill her body. It was hard to find the strength to do what she planned. But she did.

When he reached for her, she grabbed his wrists and pushed them back toward the bed. Zachary's brow furrowed. She lifted herself off of him, her body awkward. She crawled off him with her feet on the floor between his.

"Ezaray?"

Her only answer was to fall to her knees. He lifted an arm to stop her, but she leaned forward, grabbing his cock at the base the same time her mouth engulfed the head.

She tasted herself on him, but his own unique wild

flavour punched through. Zachary's hand hovered in the air above her head and curses reigned from his lips.

"Fuck, Ezaray. You don't have to do this." His tone was asking for an answer, but she ignored him. She worked up and down, each time letting him hit the back of her throat. Her scalp tingled. Zachary had gripped her hair. Scared he was going to pull her off him, she gripped tighter and sucked harder.

"Jesus, little red. Okay, I'll leave you there." He released her, but she didn't let up her efforts. His cock swelled in her mouth. The thick vein throbbed against her tongue. Faint growls escaped his chest. Ezaray needed to know that she wasn't the reason he held back.

She had her warning with a quick shot of liquid before he gripped her head and held her there while he filled her mouth. Ezaray swallowed and kept doing it as he continued to come. He released her head.

Satisfaction filled her as she lifted, sucking along the way. She licked her lips as she met his eyes.

"Little red won."

Still panting, Zachary chuckled, the sound hoarse. "Yes, she did." He reached down and wrapped his hands around her waist to pull her up. He kissed her, surely tasting the mixture of him and her. Zachary supped, licked, and nipped leisurely, in no rush. And neither was she. Confidence fizzled under her contentment.

She felt ready to begin a whole new life, but she didn't think she could do it without Zachary. That didn't bother her like it should.

CHAPTER 16

Zachary didn't sleep, but Ezaray did. She slept in his arms while he listened to Maggie in the kitchen downstairs.

He couldn't believe what Ezaray had done, never expecting her to take that kind of control and demand he find his release. His little mate had blown his mind when she latched on with more force when he was about to pull her away. Zachary wouldn't deny her with that determination.

Looking down at her, he brushed her hair back from her forehead. Her eyes fluttered open.

"Hi."

"Hi, lovely."

"You know, Red conquering the wolf is a much better ending to the story than the one with the huntsman."

"I couldn't agree more." He wanted to take her again, felt the need building inside him, but he didn't trust himself. "We should go help Maggie with lunch."

"Yes, we should." Her voice lacked the disappointment he sensed in her.

They got up, dressed, and went downstairs. Maggie was in the middle of cutting vegetables.

"What are you making? Can we help?"

Maggie glanced over her shoulder, her eyes landing on Zachary behind Ezaray as they came in. She didn't answer Ezaray, but she instead handed over the chopping and started something on the stove.

Zachary walked around the house and the outside of the house while they made lunch. He didn't expect Tyrone to find them here. There was no logical trail that connected Zachary to Alder Ridge. But he would still monitor things as the days passed. As he came back around to the front, Shaye's black truck pulled in the driveway. He met her at the front of her truck.

"How are they settling in?"

"Okay, I guess."

"Do you think they'd mind if I came in?"

"It's your house." He stepped back and let her go first. They walked into the kitchen and both women turned around. Maggie took a step back, bumping into the counter and Ezaray looked at Zachary before turning her eyes back on Shaye.

"Hi. I'm Shaye." Shaye stepped forward, but didn't reach out to either of them. "I just wanted to check in on both of you. Make sure there wasn't anything more you needed."

"I'm Ezaray and this is Maggie. Is this your house?"

"It is. It's been sitting here empty for a little while. I've been unsure what to do with it. So I'm glad it was here when you guys needed it. You're both welcome to stay as long as you need."

"That's very generous. Thank you."

"You're welcome. I left my number on the fridge when I stocked the place for you. Call anytime you need anything."

Shaye turned to Zachary. "Do you have time after lunch today to stop by the office?"

"I could." He didn't quite snarl.

"Diana has questions, then we can start our search."

"Can't you answer them?" He raised his brow, hoping to avoid such meetings and stay away until he decided what house or land to buy.

"Not for her. She must hear it from the client themselves." Her lips twitched as she mimicked her boss. Shaye patted his arm and left, giving a wave to the girls.

"Looks like I have an appointment to make after lunch, but then I'll take you two shopping for new clothes that fit and anything else you might need."

Ezaray smiled and Maggie only nodded. Zachary didn't want to have any meeting, but he couldn't deny the spark of excitement at finding his own home.

ZACHARY SAT across from the realtor Shaye worked for. Diana sat behind her desk with unnaturally impeccable posture as she grilled Zachary on what he was looking for. Her frustrations grew and tiny twitches began in her face. He wasn't being helpful with his answers. Or she didn't like them.

Shaye sat in on the meeting and he noticed her covering her lips more often than not.

"Look, all I want is something secluded. House or just land, it doesn't matter. If the house doesn't suit but the land does, then I'll change the house, but I can't change the land."

"Well, if you could tell me what you're looking for in a house, I can get you everything you're looking for and save you the trouble." She wanted to offer him everything, eager for the high-ticket sale.

"What trouble? I don't know what I want in the house and I don't care."

"Diana?" Shaye leaned forward. "I think I know what to look for, if you'll leave it with me to put a few houses together for him to look at."

Diana looked flustered, and she pulled back at Shaye's suggestion, but then she caved. "Okay. We'll sit down together to go over some listings." She stood. "We'll be in touch as soon as we have some ready for you, Mr. Hall."

"Thank you." He shook Diana's hand and let his lips twitch as he shook Shaye's.

Rolling his shoulders, Zachary stretched his muscles as he left the office and walked toward his bike. Getting on, he realized he couldn't take both girls shopping at the same time. Guess he needed to call in a favour. He pulled out his phone before he got on his bike.

"Hey Asher. Can I borrow your truck for the afternoon?"

"I'll need it back to go home."

"Will you really?" Zachary knew damn well Asher would have no problem shifting somewhere and running home. "Besides, I'll leave my bike there."

"You're kidding, right?"

"What? Are you too good to ride a motorcycle?" The jibe toward his friend came quick on his tongue.

"Asshole. Yeah, come get it."

Zachary parked outside Morestead Veterinary Clinic and walked in, going straight to the counter. "I'm looking for Asher."

"Do you have an appointment to see Dr. Morestead?" She leaned over the counter. "Or a pet?"

Zachary's first instinct was to sneer at the judgment

leaching from Asher's secretary, but he held back. Asher came through the back door behind the desk, holding up his keys.

"Does Ezaray have a problem with the bike?" Asher was unsuccessful at keeping his face straight.

"No, but I can't fit more than one extra person on there."

"Ah, I see."

The secretary had sat back down and was looking between the two men smiling at each other. Zachary never enjoyed putting someone in their place. All he wished for was that people wouldn't react to the way he looked, or whatever it was about him that made them assume he was bad news.

"If you can have it back in two hours, I'd appreciate it."

"I'll do my best. Thanks."

"Friday night?" Asher asked. Zachary knew he was asking for them to all meet out at the building. Meetings of one sort or another for them to catch up.

"Sure." Zachary left, feeling out of place in the other wolf's truck. Driving back to Shaye's, he found the girls waiting for him in the living room. He held the door and let them out first.

Shopping was painful. Neither of them were willing to buy anything. And they were both uncomfortable in the public setting. He took them to the back and asked an associate to help get their sizes.

After making them try on a couple pieces to make sure they fit, he gave a list of what to get each of them. Jeans, t-shirts, sweaters, underwear and socks. Three of each for each girl and to just ring it up. He'd already paid and was ushering the girls back out of the store before they realized what he'd done.

"The only thing you don't have are bras. If you want

those, you must get comfortable shopping on your own." Maggie scowled at his gruffness while Ezaray giggled.

A cool wind rushed through the street. It had a grey tinge and a smoky shape, but it disappeared. He froze on the sidewalk, staring after it. It gave Zachary the urge to run into the woods. He'd learned not to ignore those urges or signs, not to ignore the wind when he saw it. He wanted to bring Ezaray with him, but that would leave Maggie alone.

Zachary drove them home and went to exchange Asher's truck for his bike. Winter would be here soon, and he'd have to go back to Hull Creek to get his own truck.

Arriving back at the house, he found them both upstairs sorting through what he'd bought them. Maggie came out and met him in the hall, although her eyes wouldn't look at him. She'd turned her pink face down toward the floor.

"I'll pay you back."

He thought for a moment on the best way to respond to her. He didn't sense any determination in her, only fear. "No." He made sure the denial was clear and cutting.

Maggie's face lifted half an inch, but she kept her gaze down. The pink tinge to her skin turned red.

"You can pay it forward. You can keep it for yourself, building the life you deserve. But I won't let you pay it back."

She backed up.

"Maggie." She stopped. "You don't deserve to be put in that position, and I didn't buy those things for you and Ezaray to put either of you in that position. You just need a little boost to get back on your feet."

Shining eyes met his and her mouth formed the words *Thank you* without making a sound.

"One more thing before you go. I'm leaving again for the rest of the afternoon and overnight. I'm taking Ezaray with me. Do you want me to get someone to come stay with you?"

"I'm fine."

"You were scared last time we left."

She frowned. "I was, but I'm less scared alone."

"How about I send someone to come check up on you?"

"Okay."

"I'll ask Shaye and Nathan. You met Nathan during the rescue."

Maggie nodded and retreated to her room. When Zachary turned around, Ezaray stood just inside her bedroom door swiping a tear from her cheek.

"You've been misunderstood your whole life, haven't you?" She spoke softly as she leaned her head against the door frame.

"The legacy of a deadbeat biological father followed me growing up. After a while, I just rolled with it." He'd accepted it and stopped caring. At least, he told himself he didn't care.

"And by doing that, you've developed a dark exterior. It's all a surface impression."

"Do you want to come with me?"

"Yeah." She described him with a dark exterior and yet she accepted him as he was.

Zachary helped her pack a small bag. He called Nathan while he waited for Ezaray to say bye to Maggie. Then they were on their way toward Asher's to hike into the wilderness that was calling him.

RIDING on the back of a wolf was a surreal experience, and she hoped it became a normal thing for her. Ezaray wanted to stay a part of this life and this world. No matter what direction she took her life in from here, as long as she was still a part of all this, she could be happy.

They stopped outside the building and the same two wolves came running over the ridge, but it wasn't with excitement this time. Zachary shifted and froze, staring in their direction, but not at them. Ezaray looked. A grey swirl spun in circles in the air. It looked just like the magic that took over Zachary when he shifted.

"What's that?"

"The wind. My wind."

The wind spun and moved up and down before it shot itself to the trees and dispersed.

"Something or someone is coming. We need to stay here. Fuck, I hope it's Holly."

"How do you know that?"

"Just a feeling. The wind always shows up when it needs to warn us about something. We never know what, but we can figure it out. Instinct I guess."

They went inside and Zachary found a pair of jeans. Ezaray turned back and saw the other two wolves standing guard, their sharp eyes searching the ground and the trees. A moment later, she heard hammering coming from inside. Zachary was on edge. His frustration visible around him. She found something she could work on and decided not to bother him for now. Who knew how long they'd have to wait.

Zachary sighed and dropped the hammer. The thud on the floor echoed in the empty room. "I hate waiting." He rolled his neck and looked over at her. His lips pinched, but then broke out into a grin. "You have that piece sideways."

"I do?" Ezaray looked at the two pieces she was putting together and tilted her head. If that wasn't a square it was damn close. Zachary came over and pressed a button on the drill and pointed back at the screws. Frowning, Ezaray used the drill, and the screws came out. Zachary helped her turned the pieces and position them the right way. "Thank you."

"No problem. You did the rest of this section right." He'd crouched on the floor with one knee down and one up, and still he towered over her, trapping her in the heat and power that flowed from him.

Feeling brave, she pushed herself to her knees and moved closer. Zachary's eyes followed her while the rest of his body stilled. She laid her hands on his bare chest.

"What are you doing, little red?"

"I'm sure there are other things we can do while we wait." She didn't sound as brave as she'd intended, but she enjoyed the smirk on his face.

"There are a lot of things we could do." He rested his hands on her hips. "Who's catching who this time?" With the way his fingers flexed against her and his muscles twitched up his arms and over his chest, Ezaray saw what decision he wanted her to make.

"I think it's okay for the wolf to catch me." She might have said it, but she wasn't prepared for the force of him as he claimed her mouth. His hands moved to her ass and pulled her against him. The length of his cock sat against her pelvis as he brought her between his knees. She'd be flat on her ass if he didn't hold her. She had no purchase with her hands or on her own knees.

"You stop me if you need to," he said against her lips, not pulling away from her. Running his lips over her jaw and down her neck, he nipped and licked, sending instant rows of shivers down her centre. One hand ran up her back and through her hair, his fingers keeping contact with her head. With a growl, he fisted her hair and pulled her head to the side. His nipping turned sharp. Ezaray was running out of breath.

He cursed and pulled his face from her neck. He pushed off one foot and moved himself behind her. After pulling her sweater over her head, he pulled down the leggings she wore until they reached her knees and touched the uncovered wooden floor. One large hand covered the back of her neck and he slowly pushed on her. She followed his direction and landed on her palms.

"Further," he said harshly while he continued to push. Ezaray lowered to her elbows, and he stopped. She heard the zipper on his jeans. Her insides clenched at nothing, waiting for him to fill her.

His head prodded at her entrance. As soon as he settled it there, he thrust in one steady motion. The position was tighter than before. He stretched her, but instead of pain it only increased the pleasure. His fingers dug into her hips and her entire body soared.

"Fuck, you're already quivering. You're ready aren't you, little red?"

"Oh, yes." And she hoped he gave in this time. Her body waited, waiting for him. His hand reached around her and found her clit. She took only a moment to let the pleasure from that touch flow, but as soon as she felt her peak rising, she let out a cry. "No!"

His fingers loosened enough that she bolted forward and leaned on her hip, turning to look at him. She almost cried at the loss of him inside her, but she refused to take anything more from him without him getting what he needed in return.

"What's wrong, Ezaray?" His hands were fists hanging in the air and his breathing was harsh.

"Not without you."

"What do you mean?" She didn't answer him, but it didn't take him long to figure it out. "Ezaray." His scolding growl only made her want him more.

"If you won't do it, then you need to tell me why."

What little showed of his eyes disappeared as he squeezed them shut. "You're not ready for this." Bitterness seeped through his words.

"I should be the one to determine that." She got the sense he was trying to protect her, but she saw no connection between that and their current predicament. Except for, "Are you worried about pregnancy?" she asked.

"No. That's not it." His eyes opened and they met hers. His body didn't relax, but he sat back on his heels. "Shifters have mates, but they don't get to choose their mate. Fate does."

Oh, God. He must already have a mate he didn't care for. If Fate chose and not him. He was cheating on his mate.

Ezaray pulled her knees closer, but didn't yet make a move to get dressed or stand. Her heart cracked, and she forced herself to listen to the rest. But she couldn't look at him.

"A certain scent that causes our senses to overload tells us we've found our mate. Everything is uncontrollable from there."

She frowned at the floor. Why would he be telling her how it happens? She didn't want to listen to that. Ezaray held up her hand to stop his explanation.

"Ezaray."

"No," she croaked and had to clear her throat. "No." Pulling herself off the floor, she put her clothes back to rights.

"You don't understand."

"It's not my place to understand. Except to understand

that you've used me after I asked you not to." She stood and walked toward the exit.

"I have not used you." His voice dropped to a deadly cadence, making her pause. But no matter what he believed, it didn't change what he'd done.

She turned her head to look over her shoulder, but only enough to see him from the corner of her eye. Ezaray couldn't bear to look at him straight on. "You already have a mate and yet you still fucked me."

As the rumble of a deep growl began in his chest, Ezaray ran for the door.

She skidded to a halt before she reached the wolves standing guard outside. Slowing her pace, she hurried past them.

"Ezaray!" Zachary yelled from the door. She looked back. The wolves were alert and Zachary was speaking to them.

She didn't have anywhere to go and certainly no place he wouldn't find her, but she ran anyway. Just wanting some time to feel the pain he'd caused before she faced him.

CHAPTER 17

S moke scowled at Zachary, his lip twitched with the beginning of a snarl.

"Don't look at me like that. She thinks I already have a mate, not that she is my mate."

He swore the growling wolf rolled his eyes.

"Please stop her." Zachary tried not to roll his eyes in return as he threw his hand forward in the direction Ezaray ran.

Smoke nodded and waited until she was out of sight before taking off after her. Zachary sighed and followed.

He didn't understand how the hell he'd fucked that up. And in such a bad way. He'd hurt her. His lungs had seized from the pain he'd caused.

Following Smoke's trail, he slowed to move silently to listen for when Smoke found her. Her startled scream made him tense, but then she spoke.

"Zachary?" She paused.

Zachary moved in, but hid behind a tree.

"You're Smoke." He saw his wolf brother bob his head.

Smoke had grown attached to Gwen, Asher's mate, and

Zachary knew he had the same eagerness to devote himself to Ezaray.

"I'm sure he's right behind you, but I just want to be alone. I didn't think he was like that. That he would do that to me. Do that to his mate."

Smoke closed the distance between them and nudged her stomach, shaking his head against her. Then he pushed her with his nose as if to point at her. Ezaray didn't understand. She sat down and leaned against a tree, setting her forehead on her raised knees. Smoke sat beside her and rested his chin on her shoulder.

"If I had only been his mate." Her words were muffled, but he still heard them.

Zachary came out of hiding and kept his steps silent until he stood in front of her. She held her breath while he crouched down in front of her.

"Ezaray." He reached around her knees and used his finger to lift her chin. "You are my mate."

She tried to pull her chin from his grasp, but Ezaray's eyes widened as his words seemed to register.

"Me?"

"Yeah, little red. You."

"I thought... I thought you were saying..." Her breathing picked up and her words faded.

"You thought I was telling you I already had a mate." He shook his head, watching her eyes follow his. "No, you're it."

"I still don't understand. Why won't you...?" She trailed off and lifted a hand in a weak gesture.

"I don't have enough control to do that and not do what makes the mating permanent."

"You don't want this, do you?" This time she succeeded when she jerked her chin from his grasp. Smoke lifted his head to stare at Zachary, but he never left Ezaray's side. Exactly how it should be.

"I want you more than anything. But I won't do something that you don't want. And you have known none of this world."

"You said you don't get to choose. Do I?" She'd calmed with a slow analytical tone.

"Not from what I've seen."

"Then why fight it? If there's no choice because this is what's meant to be, then there's no point. Everything will work out the way it's supposed to. Right?"

Her confidence floored him. "You have that kind of trust in the world? After what you've been through?"

"I shouldn't." Ezaray shrugged.

"I can't take this back if I do it." He had to warn her. Armed with the truth rather than her misconception, she accepted this fate with such ease.

"I won't want you to."

Zachary braced his arms under her legs and back. He stood, cradling her against his chest. He heard the voice in his head chanting. *Mate. Mine. Mark.* It coursed through his blood uncontrollably. Now that he had her permission, his body, the animal inside him, knew what was about to happen. The pleasure hummed, ready to burst free.

He carried her back to the building, barely aware of Smoke trailing behind them. He laid her on the same bare mattress as last time and pulled at her clothes until she lay beautifully naked. All his senses tuned to a hyper-focused state aimed at Ezaray. Her arousal that had faded when she ran came roaring back as he stroked, licked, pinched until she writhed on the bed. Zachary inhaled, closing his eyes to enjoy the scent.

"All mine."

Her breath shuddered. Zachary lowered himself between her legs, and this time he didn't worry about holding back. Starting out long, slow, and forceful, he didn't take long to pick up the pace, building the most out of this connection as he could. He touched his forehead to hers, loving each sound that came from her.

"Come for me, little red. Cause I can't wait to come with you."

And there it was. Her walls gripped him tight, contracting in waves and pulling his orgasm free. Zachary's teeth had lengthened long ago. He buried his face in her neck and let an instinct he didn't understand take over. Biting her smooth flesh between her shoulder and throat, he felt their orgasms extend and take on a new life. Ezaray bucked wildly beneath him as she cried out his name.

As they came down from their high, Zachary licked and kissed the mark into a slim crescent, then collapsed beside her.

"My mate," he murmured and pulled her closer.

"What does that make you?" Even when sleepy, she turned it all around on him. He only had the energy to chuckle rather than come up with a clever answer.

EZARAY GROANED at being pulled from her sleep, but when she saw Zachary sitting alert on the bed, she ended her protests.

"What is it?"

"Get dressed." Zachary jumped up. He pulled on his jeans and grabbed a t-shirt from the bag by the bedroom door. He only waited long enough to see her grab her clothes, and he ran outside.

Whatever or whoever the wind had warned them about was here.

Ezaray pulled on her clothes quickly and ran after him. When she walked outside, she froze. Coloured winds shook frantically in the air and Zachary stared up in the trees. Two owls sat staring at him.

"Please, Holly. Come down." Zachary called out with a slightly higher pitch to his deep growl. The sound of him begging hurt Ezaray.

One owl flew down to the ground, shaking. Without a graceful landing, she braced herself on a wing. Then magic happened. All similar to what she'd seen with Zachary, but more of it. The transition for Holly looked smoother, until the end. The shaping of a human body looked much more painful.

After the shift, Holly stood naked, shaking, drowsy, and unstable. She fell forward, but Zachary moved quickly to catch her. Her hands clutched at his shirt while he held her. Ezaray moved closer. She heard Zachary soothing her with soft words.

"I've got you, Squirt. You're safe." He continued to croon and shush her until the shaking stopped, and even then he didn't let her go. Ezaray felt as if she was intruding. She wasn't part of the relationship they'd had, their special bond in childhood. She started to back up, but Zachary stopped her. "Don't go anywhere, little red."

The winds had gone, and a calmness settled in the trees. Zachary continued to stroke Holly's hair and back. Ezaray knew he wouldn't move until Holly was ready.

She pushed on his chest.

"I needed to see you. But I'm not ready for this like I thought I was. I'm not ready to be here. I want to go." Her words rushed together in a broken chorus. Her knuckles turned white as she looked up, pleading with Zachary. Ezaray didn't need to be close to see the tears in her eyes. Holly rarely cried. Even when they were captives.

"Holly, you don't need to be alone for any of this. You don't have to go home. You don't even have to go in public. But please, don't leave on your own." She looked up at Zachary and as if just sensing Ezaray for the first time, her head slowly turned.

"Zee?"

Ezaray stepped closer.

"What are you doing here? Why didn't you go home?"

"Not without you. We go home together." Ezaray closed the rest of the distance, needing the contact of her best friend.

Holly's nose twitched and she shook her head.

"There are some things you don't yet know about being a shifter." Zachary soothed as if he would spook a wild animal.

Holly frowned up at Zachary.

"You know I've found other shifters. They're good people, and we're all learning." He was trying to coax her into staying, but Ezaray knew it wouldn't work on Holly.

"What did you do to Zee?" Holly's lips didn't move as she spoke. Even weak as she was, she still threatened the large predator holding her.

"I haven't hurt her and it's not what you think." Zachary tried to keep a hold of her, but she pushed fully out of his reach.

"It's okay, Holly. I'm okay." Ezaray extended her arm. Holly didn't pull away, but all she allowed was for Ezaray to grab her hand.

"I can explain it all to you. I felt the same when I first came across this."

Holly grabbed her head with her free hand. She wobbled with another step she took further from Zachary. "No, I don't want to know." Holly looked at Ezaray. "Promise me you're okay."

"I promise."

"Good." She pulled her hand from Ezaray's. Popping sounds echoed, but didn't last long before wind swirled around Holly. Definitely a different experience for her than it was for Zachary.

"Holly, don't." Zachary rasped as he lunged to reach for her.

Her transformation didn't stop.

"Stay close." Zachary called into the air as the beautiful owl took flight and the second, still perched in the tree, followed her. "Fuck." His loud curse dropped under the swish of their wings.

For long moments, Zachary stood with his head tilted back, following their trail as long as he could then he continued to search the trees and the sky that peeked through.

Unable to judge his reaction, Ezaray chanced laying her hands on his arm. Zachary sighed and pulled her close.

"Why did she think you hurt me?" Ezaray looked up at him until he turned his head down to her, defeat shining in his eyes.

"Once I marked you, your scent changed." The bite. She lifted her hand to her neck. "To a shifter you smell like a shifter, but not quite right. It's strange unless you know what it is."

"I'm worried about her." Her worry had only gotten worse since the escape.

"You and me both. It's hard being away from your pair for that long, but being away from your pair and unable to shift yourself would be torture." Understanding filled his words even though he turned back to search the trees.

"You say that like you know."

"I was away from Smoke for over two years." Zachary turned his head away from her, but she saw his painful wince.

Ezaray tilted her head to the sky and realized that she wouldn't be able to help her friend through this. Holly would need Zachary. Even though Ezaray would be by her side, she would have to trust and lean on him.

SOMETHING NAGGED AT ZACHARY. His life never felt easy. And yet, over the less than two weeks since they'd first seen Holly, things fell into place.

For days after she first showed up, Zachary stayed in the woods, asking Asher to drive Ezaray back and forth when she didn't spend the night. He'd searched all around the building, the pack's territory, and further, hoping to catch the scent of an owl. Only when she showed up on her own three days later, perched on the front steps of the building, had he let go of his guilt and allowed himself out of the woods.

Zachary had started bringing Ezaray with him to view houses. It would be hers too, although he hadn't asked her if she wanted to live in Alder Ridge. They'd yet to find anything they liked. Zachary was getting ready to build his own, but winter was approaching too quickly. And they still had to get Asher's safe house finished. They worked on it daily with Asher, Gwen, Nathan, and Shaye joining when they could. It was just about livable. All that was left was aesthetics.

Ezaray slowly came around to getting to know Gwen and Shaye. She'd been shy and uncertain at first, and Gwen and Shaye didn't push her. She'd also been spending time with Maggie.

Maggie had changed in such a short time. With some help from connections of Asher's and Gwen's, Maggie had applied for part-time work, jobs that would keep her out of the public eye. She wasn't ready for that. And she'd applied for funding to take some courses. She was still quiet, barely speaking two words to anyone other than Ezaray, but she'd come a long way since they'd arrived in Alder Ridge.

Things were moving, but Zachary had the feeling of unfinished business.

They'd spotted Holly a few times flying by. She'd stayed close like he asked. He was thankful for that. A couple times, she'd fly down to perch beside him or even on his shoulder. He took those times to talk to her, to tell her all he'd learned about being a shifter since he met Asher, about mates, and bits and pieces of life since she moved away as a little girl.

Holly would do the same with Ezaray and when she did, Ezaray would walk off further into the woods to talk in private. Zachary didn't try to follow or intervene. He wouldn't take the privacy away from either of them.

He'd checked in with Garrett twice a day. He still had a tail on him, but he felt the threat of being discovered as involved had passed. Although, Garrett didn't feel safe to divulge any specifics over the phone.

While Ezaray was off with Holly, Zachary called Garrett himself. He wanted to see him in person and to get clear information on anything he knew about Tyrone. It was time to put it all to rest. Not that they hadn't been watching the news. Stories of an illegal organization getting shut down ran through the news for about a week, but details had been vague. They hadn't seen or heard anything since.

"Dr. Garrett Daly," he clipped a professional answer as Zachary had called his work cell.

"I'd like to make an appointment at your earliest convenience. A house call." Zachary hoped he understood what he was asking. They never said anything over the line that could point fingers at either of them in the case Tyrone had his phones bugged.

"Of course. I'll get back to you with an appointment as soon as I can." Garrett disconnected the line.

Ezaray came back, Holly flying over and around her. She landed on a large boulder next to Zachary. Zachary ran his knuckle over her head.

"Love you, Squirt."

Holly spread her wings and disappeared into the trees. Where she was staying with her pair, he didn't know, but as long as she continued to show up, he wouldn't worry. Yet.

Zachary pulled Ezaray into his side. "How do you think she's doing?"

"I have no idea, but she keeps coming back."

Zachary lifted her chin, tilting her head to the side. He ran his fingers down her neck and over the faint mark he'd left on her skin. He craved to make another one.

"Zachary?" She breathed his name. When he looked at her face her eyes were closed. He inhaled. Sweet cherries and the faint scent of arousal filled his nose. Damn it. They didn't have time. They had an appointment with Shaye and Diana.

Fuck it. They could be late.

He kissed her, claiming her mouth as he craved to claim her body. Pulling her against him, their bodies heated. An urgency flooded his system, one that felt filled with magic.

Zachary's control slipped. He knew this was different than the other times he'd claimed her. There was magic hovering around them.

"Ezaray." He needed to warn her. "I can't stop this."

She clutched at his shoulders and moved her body along his. "Then don't try."

He growled as he tore at her clothes, pulling her shirt over her head in a rush and pushing at her pants. Lifting her, he sealed their lips and walked to the nearby boulder. He leaned against it and turned Ezaray around in his arms, holding her back to his chest. Zachary nipped the clear skin on her neck making his teeth lengthen under the anticipation.

"Zachary, please," she pleaded through harsh panting.

He released his cock from his jeans and pulled her hips back with one hand while he angled his cock with the other. He held the tip at her entrance.

"What do you want, red?" he whispered in her ear, nipping the lobe while he waited for her answer. She whimpered. "Say it."

"You." She wiggled her hips, trying to push herself back, but he tightened his hold on her. Moisture dripped from her entrance, coating his cock.

"Not good enough. I want more. What do you want?" He demanded everything from her. Her hands gripped his thighs and she tried move in his grasp. "You're not moving until you tell me what you want."

"I want all of you and more. Please, take me, Zachary."

He pulled her down, impaling her in one motion. They both groaned as her walls clamped down around him. Running his hand up her torso, he cupped a breast then the other, twisting the peaks to hard nubs until she squirmed and whimpered in his grasp. Ezaray's muscles tightened and so did his. Their climaxes were rushing forth.

Warmth fell over them. Beautiful swirled patterns made of grey wind danced around them, stroking their skin when it got too close. Zachary moved his hand to her neck and gripped lightly, tilting her chin up.

"Do you see it?"

"Yes." Breathless wonderment.

Words that weren't his own filled his head. Ezaray cried out with her orgasm and Zachary's followed with a sudden rush.

"Blessed by the wind. Brought together by Fate. You're mine and I am yours."

"Bound and blessed. I am yours."

With his sharp teeth, he sank into her skin, creating an identical mark as before. As soon as he pierced her flesh, their pleasure stretched and pulsed into a second orgasm. Ezaray cried out and Zachary groaned as he licked and supped at her healing skin.

He held her tight as their bodies calmed and the warmth of the wind lifted away.

"That was amazing," she said sleepily as she leaned her head back against his shoulder.

"Our bond is sealed. I hope you understand what that means."

"Mmm. I understand." She leaned harder against him, not fully awake.

"Later, little red. We'll talk more later." Zachary nipped the mark on her shoulder then turned her around to kiss her awake while he helped her dress. "We have an appointment to make."

CHAPTER 18

Ezaray stayed back with Shaye while Diana complained about the house she was showing Zachary. She didn't want to show it at all, but Shaye had insisted. Zachary walked around the house, often walking away from Diana, who'd quickly clamber on her heels to catch up. Shaye was having difficulty holding in her laugh and the more she stuttered, the more Ezaray began to giggle. Unable to hold it in, they left the house to wait outside.

After about fifteen minutes more of looking around, Zachary popped out the front door.

"Ezaray." He gestured for her to come back in. Shaye came forward too and stopped Diana from following them into the house. "What do you think? What do you see?"

"I see a lot of space." Anything that wasn't broken or cracked was out of date. Only someone with enough determination would want to turn this place around. But every room was huge. Three bedrooms, two bathrooms, and no basement. It was nestled down a lonely lane on the opposite side of the ridge from Asher's, still hiking distance to the pack. She'd discovered she craved the seclusion as much as Zachary.

"And?" Zachary prompted.

"I see a new kitchen island, dark stained cupboards. And some work to the brick around the fireplace." She cringed at the stains and the old colours. She looked up at Zachary. The smile on his face was utter joy. So much light through his dark features.

"Do I buy it?"

She nodded. The house would be perfectly charming when they finished with it.

"Ezaray, we haven't talked about this yet, but I want you to live with me in Alder Ridge." He stepped closer and wrapped his hands around her wrists, waiting for her response.

"Well, yeah." She frowned. "Where else would your mate live?"

He kissed her quick and harsh then lifted his head back and yelled for Diana.

"Yes, Mr. Hall?" Her heels clicked on the floor as she watched each step she took. Once she stopped, she lifted her head to meet Zachary's eyes.

"Get the paperwork ready, please. I'm putting in an offer."

"Are you serious?" Her professionalism that she seemed to hold so tight dropped for a moment. Zachary's joyful face turned into a dark scowl that he aimed directly at Diana. "Of course." Her tone and posture changed instantly. "Let's head back to the office."

After an exciting kiss, Zachary dropped Ezaray off to see Maggie before going in to sign the paperwork for the offer.

She walked in and found Maggie in her usual spot, reading on the couch. Only a second of fear flashed on her face now when someone walked in. Although, Ezaray and Zachary had technically been staying here too, they did spend most of the time camping at the building while they worked on it. Ezaray was proud of the work she was doing to help. She wasn't terrible at it and she found she enjoyed it. What she would do with that information, she didn't know.

"Did you get the job?" Ezaray sat across from Maggie.

"Yup. I start tomorrow." Maggie had applied as a housekeeper at one of the local bed and breakfasts. She'd only been applying for one job at a time, too scared to put herself out there.

"Congratulations." Ezaray patted Maggie's knees.

"Thanks."

"Are you thinking of staying in Alder Ridge even after you feel like you're on your feet?"

"I think so. Shaye even said I could rent this house for whatever I could afford until I really know what I want."

Maggie and Ezaray seemed to be opposite in their healing. Maggie hadn't settled until she started to get her feet under her, but Ezaray settled first and had yet to figure out what to do from here. It was hard without seeing her family yet or going home with Holly.

"I'm still scared." Maggie's whisper cut through her thoughts.

"Of what?"

"Of my old life. I worry I'll end up back there." Maggie picked at something imaginary on the back of her hand.

Ezaray stayed quiet even though she wanted to ask. She'd learned by now that if Maggie wanted to say something, she'd only say it on her own terms.

"I've always been controlled. This is the first time I've ever made a decision for myself."

"Then we'll make sure it stays that way." Ezaray set her

hand on her knee and was rewarded with a small smile. Alder Ridge was good for both of them.

ZACHARY DIDN'T WANT Ezaray here for the meeting, or to have Holly nearby, but as the other mates showed up with Asher and Nathan, he didn't have a choice. The scent of an owl flew down with the wind. He couldn't see her, but she was watching and listening. Now, they only waited for Garrett.

Thankfully, the wait wasn't long.

One hawk perched in a tree and another flew down to the ground. Asher's face as Garrett shifted was just as Zachary imagined it would be. He was fascinated. Shifting for the birds, and Zachary assumed any smaller animal, took more magic.

Zachary tossed Garrett the jeans he held for him.

"There wasn't really time for a proper introduction before. This is Garrett Daly, hawk shifter and doctor." Nods and introductions followed as they each introduced themselves and their mates. Garrett looked to the sky and nodded at something the rest of them couldn't see. He must know where Holly was perched.

"Has she shifted again?" he asked.

"No." Zachary answered, but didn't want to continue to talk about Holly when she was listening in. "I hope you have more information than what the news was reporting."

"I do. All the guys you handed over to the police are still in custody, but don't expect it to last much longer. The building has been searched so they know exactly what was happening, but there's no evidence to point to who, except some of the betting clients who've lawyered up and will be fine, I'm sure."

"Tyrone?"

"Sill loose and still has more than a handful of people with him. I'm sure he'll rebuild."

"Didn't any of those guys roll over on him?"

"Sort of. Some of them gave names, although I doubt it was any of the guards. The problem is they all gave different names or multiple names. They've got nothing."

"Has Tyrone called you?"

"Only to hang up on me. It's his way of telling me he's still around and watching. I've seen his guards and new ones watching my apartment and the hospital where I work. I'm not free of him."

"You would be if you disappeared."

"But if he ever found me, whoever he finds beside me will also be in danger. I can't take that chance." The damn noble hawk. His animal and profession suited him well.

"You're welcome here whenever you need." Asher spoke up. "That's the purpose of all this." He gestured to the almost finished building behind him.

"So I've heard. Thank you."

"Do you know what Tyrone is planning? Will he come after us?" Ezaray spoke from beside him. A faint whoosh had all the shifters looking up. Holly had perched closer to hear Garrett's answer.

"I don't know. I think for the moment he's only focusing on rebuilding. If he was interested in fighters again, it would be easier to start new, but he had an obsession with his strongest fighters."

All three of which now resided in Alder Ridge.

"If I find out anything, you'll all be the first to know." Garret looked to each of them.

It wasn't the closure Zachary had been hoping for, but it was the best they'd get for now. Tyrone had no reason to look in Alder Ridge.

Asher invited Garrett inside to tour the building and they all chatted from there in their usual way. Garrett fit in well, as Zachary had expected. He and Asher quickly started a conversation about shifter physiology while the rest of them started picking up tools and got to work.

Zachary looked forward to putting the same kind of work into his own house. His next task would be to find a shop to house his own motorcycle repair business. His life was coming together, but there was still one thing missing.

Seeing everyone occupied, he quietly stepped outside. He stood in the open, looking up and waiting. After a moment, Holly swooped down.

"I still miss you. You're here, but you're not. You're the last one in my family, old and new, that's missing." He reached out and she leaned her head against his hand. Her feathers were soft. "You're beautiful, Squirt. But you deserve to live a life as both an owl and a woman."

Zachary didn't need to say anymore. He'd said what he came out to. Instead, he tapped his shoulder and waited for her to hop up, then he hiked toward the pack to visit with Smoke. He should have introduced the two of them a very long time ago.

***

EZARAY HADN'T BEEN SPENDING every night with Zachary, despite that being what she wanted. Some nights she'd camp with him and others she'd stay here with Maggie. Maybe once a week, Zachary would spend the night here as well, but he was most content near the pack.

He'd told her about his separation from his wolf brother, his pair. The terms were interchangeable. Not growing up as a society of their own, their culture was still forming. As a mate, she was part of that. Getting to know Gwen and Shaye was helping her to understand many things, mostly about her own feelings toward Zachary. Gwen was forming a legend, a collection of the stories of the shifters they meet and all the things they learn along the way. Ezaray didn't believe what she had to say was much help, but both Gwen and Shaye had listened intently before telling her their experiences.

Making new friends made her miss Holly. Seeing her in her owl form helped. She knew who she was. But her friend was damaged, not willing to come back to herself to heal.

If Holly didn't come around soon, Ezaray didn't know how much longer she could wait for her best friend until she moved on with her own life. She'd been making friends. Even Maggie was becoming more than just someone she'd been in captivity with. Not just a friend so she had something to call her, but a true friend. Ezaray loved watching her succeed.

She had a feeling that Maggie had had it a lot harder than any of the girls. Ezaray was proud of her. She was proud of herself, but she wanted there to be more of which to be proud.

Ezaray sat in the living room, waiting for Maggie to get home from her shift at the bed and breakfast. She hadn't said much about her job and Ezaray wanted to know if she was okay working.

She heard the key in the door and set her book down. It was such a thrill to be able to do something as simple as reading.

Ezaray almost didn't catch the startle on Maggie's face.

She was getting better. Or she was at least getting better at hiding it.

"Hey." Ezaray smiled warmly at Maggie, but stayed still on the couch.

"Hi. Have you been here long?"

"No. Zachary dropped me off a little while ago. He has more paperwork to do for the house."

Maggie set her small purse she had found in the house on the end table. Shaye had said either of them were free to use whatever they found. Ezaray hadn't used anything for herself yet. She didn't need to when she wasn't sure what she was about to do.

A hard, slow knock sounded on the door. They both froze when no one called their name. Anyone who came to check on them would call their name after they knocked.

Ezaray watched Maggie pull in a deep breath, pushing her panic down. She did the same, although her fear wasn't as great as Maggie's.

Maggie slowly opened the door, but before she could even look out, whoever was on the other side shoved hard against it, throwing Maggie down to the ground.

He walked in and slammed the door behind him. Ezaray jumped to her feet. The air she tried to breath felt like pulling in solid ice, lodging in her throat and chilling everything inside her.

Tyrone stood staring down at Maggie. It only took him a moment before he noticed Ezaray standing there.

"I had hoped Maggie would lead to some of my other fighters, but I hadn't expected her to be staying with one of them. You're not the one I'd hoped to find, but you'll do." He took a purposeful step toward her, the sound of his foot on the hard floor ominous.

He wanted to take her back to fight. He came looking for Maggie, for his best fighters. He'd be looking for Holly next.

Well, if he was looking for a fight, she'd give him one. The icy fear inside her cracked. She braced herself, but made it look like she backed away out of fear. The smug sneer on his lips told her he bought it.

He reached for her and she swung upward, hitting him in the gut. Ezaray tried to step to the side to move behind him, but he fisted her hair and stepped into her, pulling her backward to the ground.

She cried out as he crushed her on the floor with his knee. Where was Maggie? Why wasn't she helping?

Tyrone stood and dragged her by her hair toward the door. Ezaray tried to get her feet under her to relieve the pain as she tried to pry his hands from her hair. As they neared the door, she saw Maggie shaking uncontrollably on the floor, her eyes cast downward.

"Maggie," Ezaray pleaded. "Do something. Help. Run. Anything."

Tyrone chuckled as he reached for a bag sitting inside the door. He must have brought it with him and dropped it there as he charged through the door. "Maggie isn't going to do anything." He pulled out cuffs and chains from the bag, the clinking ugly in the room. He pulled on her hair to stand her up. Ezaray couldn't stop the tears forming in her eyes from the prickling pain. "She'd never hurt her brother."

CHAPTER 19

Zachary's heart thundered, pushing with all its might to get out of his chest. His lungs constricted. He needed out of that office.

Diana stopped speaking mid-sentence. He stood from the chair, pushing it over behind him. Storming from Diana's office, he found Shaye at her desk.

"Call Nathan." His voice changed and his eyes warmed. He didn't dare look back at Diana.

"Mr. Hall, is everything okay?"

Shaye stood and blocked Diana from reaching for his arm. "I'll see him out." She grabbed her purse and rushed after him. "What is it?"

"I don't know. Panic." In the middle of the street flew his grey wind. It throbbed as if it had the same breathing restrictions he did.

Ezaray.

"Call Asher too." Zachary slid his helmet on and ripped out of the parking lot. He made it to Shaye's in time to see a large sedan pull out of the driveway. He followed the car, knowing Ezaray was inside. Most likely Maggie, too. How was he going to stop the car?

Better question was how was he going to get them in the woods so he could tear, who he hoped was Tyrone, to shreds?

The tinted windows blocked his view. He couldn't see a damn thing inside, but he felt familiar eyes. His mate was looking back at him. Zachary assumed the driver spotted him because the car picked up the pace. He'd put a fortune down on the driver being one of Tyrone's guards. But how the hell did he find them? It must have been him. Nothing else made sense. There was nothing logical bringing them to Alder Ridge.

Outside of town, toward Asher's and the direction of Hull Creek, the car lurched to a stop. The driver threw open his door. Zachary couldn't believe it was Tyrone himself that stepped out. He rested his hand on the back door and watched Zachary pass before he opened it. Looking in his rearview mirror, he saw the front passenger seat was empty.

He kept driving long enough to get around the bend and reach the next lane. Pulling in, he moved his bike into the trees so it wouldn't be visible from the road and then jogged back toward the car.

Ezaray knelt on the ground, a chain connecting her wrists to her ankles. Tyrone stood over her. She heaved as if she'd been sick. The breeze came from her direction and Zachary inhaled. No scent of vomit lingered. She hadn't been sick at all.

He didn't have to stop the car. His little mate did it for him.

"Disgusting. You were stronger than this. Who I really need is Holly."

An idea hit Zachary. He hated it. He hated using her like

that, even though she wouldn't be bait. The traffic wasn't thick, but cars and trucks passed often enough that someone would report a fight on the side of the road over girls in chains. He had no guilt over Tyrone getting taken in, but he didn't want to go in with him.

He stepped out of the trees, leaning against one in the open.

"I know where Holly is."

Tyrone's head snapped toward the trees, searching for Zachary. As soon as his eyes landed on him, he snapped his fingers. One of his guards stepped from the back seat and aimed a gun at Ezaray. Tyrone pulled one from his jacket and aimed it inside the car.

"If either of the girls move, the other dies. If you move, they both die."

"You came all this way looking for your best fighters just to kill them because someone offered you the third?"

Tyrone's eyes narrowed. "You've been to my establishment."

"A few times." Zachary shrugged with one shoulder.

"You took my girls." His entitled possession slammed his words through gritted teeth.

"I didn't take anyone."

"You think I'm stupid enough to fall for some trick. I didn't build my business by falling into traps." His spine straightened with pride at his accomplishments.

"Oh, you're definitely stupid." Zachary smirked when Tyrone growled. "But I'm not lying. I know where she is."

Eyes still on Zachary, Tyrone turned his face toward his guard. "Stay with them." He tucked his gun away and took a step toward Zachary.

"She's smarter than you. You won't find her or catch her unless she has a reason to come out of hiding."

"I thought you were going to take me to her?" Tyrone narrowed his eyes.

"You are stupid," he mumbled, but he didn't intend for Tyrone not to hear his words. "I only said I know where she is."

"You're wasting my time." Tyrone stepped back to the car, wise enough not to turn his back on Zachary.

"Am I?" Zachary ran his fingers over the stubble on his jaw. "You said yourself, you need Holly."

"Get in the car," he demanded.

Zachary shook his head. "Can't get there by car." He nodded at Ezaray. "And they can't hike with chains around their ankles."

"Too bad." He bent to peer in the car. "Get out, Maggie."

Maggie made her way out of the car, her chains slowing her down, and Tyrone pulled Ezaray to her feet. Zachary didn't disguise his growl from seeing Tyrone's hands on her. He locked eyes with Ezaray. He couldn't say anything that she would understand, and he couldn't make any gestures. But he hoped she understood his plan just from the look in his eyes.

⌁

No way in hell would Zachary give up Holly, even to save her. There was another purpose. As soon as he said they all needed to hike into the woods, she understood. He only wanted them out of sight and on shifter territory. She'd done the right thing pretending to be sick to make Tyrone stop the car. When she'd recognized Zachary following behind on his bike, she knew he wouldn't be able to stop them or continue to follow them without being noticed or getting hurt.

The hike was slow and difficult with the chains. Their weight registered after the first ten minutes. With her hands drooping lower, Ezaray's chain caught on the edge of a log. Pulling, she felt the bite of the metal against her wrists. Tyrone and his guard only stared, waiting for her to free herself. She tried backing up, but one of the chain links had jammed.

"Hurry up," barked Tyrone.

Zachary growled. To Tyrone and the guard, it looked like he growled at her as he yanked her chain free with frustration. He quickly went back to his position ahead of them to lead them through the woods.

Ezaray didn't recognize anything, but Zachary hadn't taken her farther than the pack's territory. She'd recognized the road they'd left town on. It was the direction of Asher's. These woods must connect to his.

"How did you get in?" Tyrone filled with self-righteous superiority. A trait that terrified her before seemed disgusting now.

"In where?" Zachary was playing dumb.

"Into my club. You couldn't just walk in." He spoke with the same tone he'd used when warning the girls of their actions. Low and careful through straight lips.

"That's exactly what I did. Your guards can't see past an act for the life of them." Zachary kept hiking.

"You're lying."

"Afraid not." He lifted one shoulder in a shrug before veering around a tree.

Having less than perfect staff would piss him off. Ezaray never thought to ask how Zachary got in. She'd assumed the doctor helped him from the beginning.

She glanced up at Tyrone and saw his jaw working back and forth, grinding his teeth together.

The thing that concerned Ezaray the most about Zachary's plan was the guns. Each man had one, and she couldn't be sure if those were the only weapons. She doubted even a shifter could survive getting shot.

Ezaray didn't want anyone to get hurt because of her. And the last thing she thought she'd be able to live through would be the loss of Zachary.

She turned her eyes to the ground to hide her useless tears. Maggie's feet appeared in her line of vision beside her. Ezaray had to think past her fear and anger to sort through what she'd learned about Maggie.

It would be simple to blame Maggie, name her a traitor for leading her brother here. Tyrone was her brother. Maggie was too frightened by the littlest things to be the partner of a villain like Tyrone. What kind of life had Maggie lived?

But somehow, Tyrone had tracked her here.

"Maggie." Ezaray had hidden her tears and tried to get Maggie's attention.

Maggie turned her head away and slowed her pace so she walked behind Ezaray.

"I know you didn't do this."

"Of course she didn't. She might be a damn good fighter, but she isn't capable of anything else. She doesn't even speak for fuck's sake." Tyrone jerked on Maggie's chains.

Zachary's step paused as he listened, but he covered his hesitation by moving debris out of the way unnecessarily.

"Your brother controlled your life, didn't he?" Ezaray was unsure of Tyrone's full wrath. He'd always been so controlled, so careful not to harm his fighters. She wasn't one of his fighters right now and his organization lay in pieces. He was unpredictable.

Tyrone froze and stepped in front of Ezaray. The air

darkened around him. "You could learn some things from Maggie. You are best when you're silent."

"What is she talking about?" Zachary sounded closer.

Tyrone half turned, tilting his head around. Zachary had moved in a few feet behind Tyrone, his arms crossed over his chest. Tyrone's half smile was one Ezaray feared, and by Maggie's flinch, she did too.

Zachary didn't look at her.

"You care for her. Or is it my little sister you care for? Taking my girls wasn't just some noble act." He faced off with Zachary. Tyrone's brows lifted as Zachary stood completely still.

"Your little sister?"

"Step-sister, really. My father, long past his prime became friendly with a beautiful young mother. He cherished his new two-year-old daughter until his death. Then she became mine."

"What happened to her mother?" The only sign of Zachary's anger was the scratch to his voice.

"I kept her too, but she died years ago." Tyrone didn't sound like he missed her.

Ezaray's stomach rolled. She may have faked being sick to stop the car for Zachary, but what Maggie must have lived through made it real. Swallowing it down, Ezaray balled her fists together in front of her. She lunged forward, jabbing Tyrone in the centre of his spine. He collapsed to the ground and she followed him down as snarls and roars emerged from the shadows.

Her chains jerked to the side, smashing her into the ground. She blinked when her head hit a tree root sticking up. Her vision blurred and the figures around her twisted together making it impossible for her to understand what was happening. Ezaray started this. Now she hoped she didn't cause the death of someone she loved.

HAVING TRAVELLED FAR ENOUGH into the woods, Zachary had no trouble stopping when Ezaray spoke. But what she said, he hadn't been prepared for. Maggie was Tyrone's sister. It hadn't been Zachary that led him to Alder Ridge after all. Tyrone hadn't even recognized him right away. He'd tracked his sister. But how? Ezaray defended Maggie. She hadn't betrayed them.

Listening to Tyrone wave his authority as if he owned them all had rage filling his gut at a steady pace. Zachary sniffed the air. Wolves and bears approached.

They wouldn't get out of this, but Tyrone and his guard were still armed and too close to the girls.

Zachary's heart plunged deep when Ezaray's face hardened. She cried out and shoved herself forward. Just in time for the shifters and their pairs, including Smoke, burst through the thick forest.

The guard pulled his gun while the animals surrounded him. Tyrone reached behind him and yanked on Ezaray's chains throwing her to the side. Maggie had tripped and now sat on her knees frantically looking at everything around her. The same terror at the sight of Tyrone echoed when she looked at the animals snapping and snarling, prepared to attack.

Zachary took a step toward Ezaray, but froze as Tyrone's gun came into view as he stood with slow movements.

"I don't know what kind of fucking circus you have, but call them off." This man wasn't afraid. His guard was terrified, but Tyrone's assurance gave him perceived power.

"I don't control them," he said, not hiding even an ounce of judgment toward the other man.

"She dies. Then you. And I'll leave here with my sister." They looked at Maggie, who shivered on the ground, barely audible whimpers escaping.

Zachary made a show of counting the animals, his finger in the air. "And one, two." He pointed at the guard and Tyrone. "I don't think you'll make it out of here."

A sad smile crept across Tyrone's lips as he cocked the gun pointed at Ezaray. The man really had wanted to leave here with his fighters. But he wouldn't go back on his word.

Zachary sensed her too late. The screech chilled the air. Tyrone swung, not paying attention to where he pointed the gun. He looked up in time for Holly to attack his face. As her claw dug into his eye, the gun fired.

The bears attacked the guard, hitting his arm a second before he fired his gun.

Tyrone dropped his gun and his hands swung toward Holly. Zachary moved in and stopped one hand from punching her, but his other had grabbed at her legs. The sickening crack almost stopped Zachary, but he had to take Tyrone down. Reaching across his body, Zachary gripped Tyrone's wrist, cracking it the same he just did to Holly.

His maniacal cry increased and he let go of Holly. She flapped frantically to get away.

Tyrone swung with his uninjured arm, surprisingly adept in his condition. Blood filled his eye and poured from the socket. Scratches sliced his face. Zachary blocked and followed through with his own punch, forcing Tyrone back toward the waiting wolf behind him.

Smoke's snarl would scare even him if he didn't know better. Tyrone lost his footing. Smoke leapt, locking his jaw on Tyrone's neck. The rest of his life only lasted seconds.

Panting, Zachary took stock. Ezaray lay on the ground, blinking rapidly, but she was alert and trying to focus. Shifters and pairs stood around the dead guard. And Maggie lay on the ground, unmoving.

Fuck.

Asher shifted and ran to Maggie. Nathan shifted and stood ready for whoever needed him.

Zachary knelt beside Ezaray.

"Red? Are you okay?" He gently stroked a hand across her forehead.

"My head hurts. But I'm okay." She sounded as if she'd just woken up from a deep sleep.

"Red?" Nathan asked.

Zachary ignored him, but it only took a second before the grumpy bear shifter chuckled.

Two hawks soared in, chasing the wind, with Holly's pair following behind them. Garrett began his shift before he hit the ground. His bare feet landed and he rushed to take over for Asher to save Maggie.

"Is anyone else injured?" he called, not looking up.

"Ezaray, but she's alert and not bleeding. And Holly, broken leg."

"The rest?"

"Are dead." Asher answered for them.

Zachary looked over at Nathan and shrugged. "Oops." He may not have intentionally planned on killing them, but he held no remorse.

Nathan's brow quirked. Neither did he.

Warmth filled the space. Each shifter searched around them, except for the doctor. His focus never left his patient.

She stood off in the distance, the winds, more of them now, hovered, frozen around her. The ghost from the past looked on with a sad smile, but pride in her eyes as she nodded at each of the shifters and then their pairs.

Seeing Holly's wind alongside the rest had Zachary jerking his head around. During the fight he didn't see where Holly had gone. His eyes searched the trees and the ground. Her pair flitted from branch to branch, eyes darting everywhere. Holly was gone. She was injured and she'd fled.

"Holly's missing." They all looked around.

"Maggie will be fine, but she needs a hospital." Garrett stood. Asher stayed with Maggie while the doctor came to check on Ezaray. After looking her over, feeling her head, and searching her eyes, he nodded. "Just a good bump on the head. You'll be okay after a lot of rest."

They turned at the sound of a loud crack. Asher held up broken chains and pulled the rest away from Maggie's body.

Zachary bent and with considerable force, broke Ezaray's chains.

"Time to get you somewhere safe while we clean up and find Holly." Zachary looked up at Nathan who nodded. They had his help.

The danger was dead, but they weren't out of the woods yet.

SMOKE HAD INSISTED on carrying Ezaray away from the violence. His fierceness made her smile. He was her protector while Zachary and the others dealt with the mess. Garrett took Zachary's clothes and phone, and carried Maggie to the road to meet the ambulance. The other three men shifted to animal form and watched Ezaray leave on Smoke's back before they did anything.

Ezaray was relieved she didn't need to see anything.

She'd seen enough as it was. The horrible sounds, guns firing, and the blood that even through her blurry vision shone clearly on Tyrone's face. Good job, Holly, but the sight was horrific.

She rested on Gwen's spare bed with Smoke by her side, his head resting on her hip. Sleep didn't stay with her, but it helped pass some of the long hours waiting for Zachary to get back.

Gwen frequently checked on her. She wasn't always asleep when she came in, but Ezaray kept her eyes closed most of the time.

Ezaray no longer knew the time or if it was still the same day when Zachary came in. He sat on the side of the bed and moved her hair back from her forehead. She allowed her eyes to open for him. While he looked at her gently, his muscles twitched, frustration still evident on his skin.

"You didn't find her, did you?"

"No. We found a trail, broken branches and brush, but we lost her scent. Asher and Nathan are still searching. Garrett is on his way back from the hospital to help search. I need to find her, but I need to be here with you too."

"You should go back."

"No. Not yet."

"What about..." Ezaray trailed off, not willing to say his name.

"Gone. No trace at all."

How easily that had been for them sent a chill down her spine. But the difference was Ezaray trusted these men to do the right thing. Tyrone should never be loose to terrorize a single soul. If the only way to do that was with his death, then so be it. She wouldn't feel bad about the events of today.

"It's all over, Ezaray." Zachary leaned down and pressed

his lips to hers, gentle and sweet. He lingered, not taking the kiss deeper. She lifted her arms around him and held on. Ezaray embraced his warmth, love, and power.

He stretched out beside her on the bed before he broke the kiss.

"As soon as we find Holly, I'll take you home to see your family."

"Holly won't be ready."

"No she won't, and I won't make her go, but it's not fair to you or your family to wait for her. She'll get there. I'll talk to her parents myself and assure them she's okay." He closed his eyes. "Assuming she is when we find her."

Her worry mirrored his, but he was right. She needed to find the rest of her closure so she could build her life alongside Zachary.

"And when we get back, we start renovations on our own home."

"I'd like that," she said softly.

"I love you, red." His gruff exclamation set her heart on fire.

"I love you too, wolf." She might not know her future, but all her chains were gone. And she knew for certain that Zachary would always be her freedom.

EPILOGUE

Only her leg was broken, but the rest of her hurt. Getting away from the chaos, she flew above to see what had happened. Maggie was shot, the guard dead, and the minutes left of Tyrone's life were ticking away. Ezaray was hurt, but awake and fine. There wasn't anything more she could do.

Holly needed to get away. She couldn't see any more pain and death.

She'd been avoiding everything real. Happy to spend time in the sky and trees with her owl. Seeing Tyrone, the chains around Zee and Maggie, brought back all that she was.

Pushing through the pain scoring her wings and ribs from Tyrone's hands, through the throbbing numbness of her leg, Holly escaped. She didn't get very high, forcing her to weave around branches, narrowly missing some, and not missing others at all.

A branch scraped across her side, pulling feathers and leaving a shallow, stinging wound.

Nausea and dizziness invaded. She needed to get back to Zachary.

Holly hated how she'd doubted him when he showed up to rescue her. Her heart had wept at the sight of him. Far from the lanky teenager he'd been. She'd prayed for him, begged the wind, if it was listening, to send for him to save her. It hadn't taken long for depression to set in when nothing happened. She'd accepted that she was a fighter for Tyrone and had let go of everything else. At least for herself. It was the only way she'd survived.

When Zachary had finally showed up, there'd been nothing left to save.

Holly's eyelids fluttered closed. She struggled to keep them open and keep herself in the air. She tried to turn around, to go back to Zachary, but she was disoriented. She wasn't going in the direction she'd thought she'd been.

It didn't matter, anyway. Her strength failed. Weakly flapping her wings, she fell to the ground, colliding with trees. She managed to steer herself toward a bush in the hopes to hide herself until Zachary came to find her. Holly had no doubt he would. She'd never doubt him again.

The sound that escaped her as she landed resembled chirps, painful squeaks as her foot hit the ground several times in her horrible landing. She crouched to the ground as close to the bush as she could. Her one leg and the ends of her wings kept her from falling to her side.

She went in and out of consciousness as she heard people approaching. This wasn't good.

"What was that?"

"I think it was a bird."

"It's an owl," they said with wonder. "It's not doing so good."

"What should we do?"

A young man who looked to be in his twenties crouched down and reached out to her. She snapped her beak as soon as his fingers were close enough.

"We don't do anything. I'll call Fish and Wildlife."

The group of three stepped back from her, but didn't leave her sight. She tried hard to stay awake, but she couldn't. The next thing she woke to was the sound of a vehicle door shutting and the low tone of men's voices.

Solid footsteps sounded over the grass.

"Thanks for the call. I'll take care of this. You enjoy the rest of your hike." The newcomer, she assumed was the Fish and Wildlife officer, sent the hikers on their way. He stalked around the bush to get sight of her before approaching.

Holly blinked rapidly to stay focused. She didn't want the care of Fish and Wildlife. She wanted to go back to Zachary.

"Hey there, beautiful thing. It's okay," he crooned, the sound helping her draw deeper breaths. He took several steps closer and she gave him a warning snap.

Don't you dare touch me.

"Shh. None of that. I'm only here to help." He continued to advance, not fazed in the least with her threat. He crouched down in front of her and tilted his head to both sides and downward, examining her without touching. He tsked. "You're not in good shape, are you sweet owl?"

Despite her fear of being caught, his voice soothed her. Holly tried to control her breathing to stay alert. His scent filtered in through the smells of the area around her. Homes of small animals, hikers' trails, vehicles not far in the distance.

But the conservation officer had a different scent. The only way she could think to describe it is the mountain air. The air she craved when she'd soar far from home, to fly as high as she could go. Musk, pine, and the wind that rushed down the mountain side. Uncontrollable dizziness swamped her. It was no longer from the pain, but mixed with it, she could no longer control her consciousness.

"It's okay. I've got you." His last soothing words dimmed as his hands reached for her. Her eyes closed. Holly only hoped oblivion didn't have as much pain.

Join my newsletter to receive special content, the most up to
date information on releases, and special promotions.
http://bit.ly/sarahurquhart

Also, visit my website at...
http://www.authorsarahurquhart.com
... to see my full book list.

Keep reading for an excerpt from **Amber Oath, Wounded
Winds Book Four.**

http://www.books2read.com/woundedwinds4

AMBER OATH

CHAPTER 1

"Hell of a day, eh, Tony?"

Anthony glanced at Morton getting into their vehicle. Nothing out of the ordinary had happened that day, but the calls had been non-stop. He turned the heat down in their too hot truck when the dry heat blasted his face. Morton had started his annual complaints about the approaching winter, and with that came burning extra gas by turning on every type of heater the truck had from the heated seats to the defroster that hit a windshield with no ice. "I'm beat." He looked forward to a cold beer with some TV.

The radio sounded and Hazel's voice from dispatch echoed in the cab. "I've got one more for you boys." Anthony picked up the receiver, inwardly wincing with acceptance that the day wasn't quite done.

"This is Anthony. What have you got, Hazel?" Hazel had been working dispatch for the past forty-five years, ever since her eighteenth birthday. They'd all heard her stories from her younger years.

"An injured owl. Some hikers called it in." She rattled off the location.

"Got it. I'm on my way." He put the receiver back and pulled away from the lake. "I'll drop you off on the way. We don't need two of us for an owl. You might as well go home."

"If you're sure. I don't mind going with you." Morton shrugged, but his shoulders had already slumped against the leather seat.

"I'm sure. It's up near my place, anyway." Morton wasn't lazy, but once he clocked out in his head, he clocked out completely.

Anthony pulled in behind Morton's truck. "See you tomorrow."

"Have a good one."

"You too." As soon as Morton closed the truck door, Anthony left, taking the road toward the edge of town closer to the mountains. He found a couple hikers bouncing to keep warm on the side of the road. The bright colours of their jackets made them look like flags waving in the wind. When they saw his white truck, they hailed him down unnecessarily. Anthony pulled to the side as much as possible without driving into the ditch and parked. "Hi there. You called about an owl?"

"Yes, we did." A slim guy wearing bright blue stepped forward.

"I'm Officer Green with Fish and Wildlife." He extended his hand, and the guy shook it.

"It's up this way." He led Anthony into the trees. "It doesn't look good. We didn't dare touch it."

"You did the right thing."

"I don't think it's been there long. Wonder what an owl is doing out at this time of day."

"Not all owls are nocturnal. Some are active at dawn and dusk, and even some are active during the day and sleep at night." Most people blanketed all owls into one category, but there were more species of owls than people realized.

"I didn't know that. It's hunkered down next to that bush." He crouched, his eyes squinting and his arm outstretched to point.

Anthony bent down. Stained white feathers poked out from around the bush. The pattern of black speckles over the oddly positioned wing told him it was a snowy owl. Not rare around here, and not nocturnal.

Anthony stood and realized he now had a group of four hikers crowding around him.

"Thanks for the call. I'll take care of this. You enjoy the rest of your hike." He watched them walk away, moving fast to warm up, then he stalked closer to the bush, moving around the side to see what he was dealing with. Blood stained her feathers on her outstretched wing and on the feathers along her side. Only one feather-clad foot touched the ground beneath her. More blood stained the underside around her legs. She was balancing precariously. Eyes that should be yellow glowed a bright orange, and she blinked at him, trying to focus. The poor thing must be in a lot of pain.

"Hey there, beautiful. It's okay," he crooned. With slow movements, he stepped closer, within reaching distance. As quick as the bird of prey she was, her head lurched and she snapped, her beak clacking together. A defensive move, lashing out in fear. She swayed from the movement. "Shh. None of that. I'm only here to help."

Anthony crouched down and tilted his head from side to side to get a good look at her. "You're not in good shape, are you sweet owl?" He'd kept his voice at a calm monotone in hopes to soothe her.

He watched her struggle while trying to figure out the

best way to go about this. He didn't want to cause more harm when he didn't know the full extent of her injuries. An injured wing and he assumed a broken foot, but with the scrape along her side, he couldn't be sure what else.

Her chest puffed in and out and her eyes fluttered. Anthony slowly stretched out his hands, but she didn't snap at him again.

"It's okay. I've got you." He caught her as she fell forward when her eyes closed. She'd lost consciousness.

He gently felt her body for more injuries before lifting her. Standing up, he cradled her uninjured side against his chest and used one hand to support underneath her. His heart ached for the pain she must be in. What she must have gone through.

There was a rehabilitation centre about two hours north and he knew she'd be well taken care of there, but he wasn't so sure she'd make it. The next best place to take her would be to Asher Morestead, Alder Ridge's resident veterinarian. When he'd passed Morestead Clinic in town, it had been closed. Anthony hoped Asher was home.

He hiked back to his truck and positioned himself in the driver's seat, continuing to cradle the owl against him. Frowning, he twisted to reach the opposite side of the steering wheel to switch gears with his left hand. He drove one-handed toward Asher's. She didn't stir until he parked his truck.

Jarring pain lanced through her. Holly woke with a gasp and found herself engulfed in large, warm hands. She tensed and looked up. Rich brown eyes filled with comfort looked down at her. The hand beneath her lifted and one finger stroked over her head. His touch, that simple gesture, took some pain away.

A breeze that should have been chilly with encroaching winter rushed around them, creating a pocket of warm air. It was her wind. The unique coloured swirl circled above her and around his head, ruffling his chestnut hair. Seeing the wind meant something. It was always a sign or a warning. But Holly didn't have the strength to decipher its meaning right now.

"I'm going to get you some help." He took a few stairs, then knocked on a door. He was the only thing in her line of sight, and she didn't want to look anywhere else. His scent filled her again as it had back in the woods. The sensations it created mixed with her pain left her floundering, drunk on a potion.

He knocked on the door. Holly recognized the voice of the man that answered.

"Hi, Tony." It was Asher, a friend of Zachary's, who'd helped them escape from the underground fighting ring and had also fought against Tyrone in the woods today.

Guilt crashed on her chest and filled her lungs, clogging the way for her to breathe. She'd fled. She'd fled like a coward. Violence had filled those moments in the woods. Holly did what she needed to do, gouged Tyrone's eye to keep him from shooting her best friends, but as soon as the danger was over she got out of there. Tyrone had broken her leg trying to get her off him. She'd regretted fleeing, trying to find her way back to Zachary, but she'd been too weak.

"Hey, I need your help. Some hikers found an injured owl, and I don't think she'll make it all the way to the rescue centre without being treated first. I hope it's okay I brought her here. I saw your clinic closed when I passed on my way out here."

"Of course it's okay. I'm glad you brought her here." Asher let them in, then started digging in a closet by the door. "In the kitchen. We'll set her down on the table."

The Fish and Wildlife officer, Asher had called him Tony, held her close and waited for Asher's instructions.

"There."

"I'm pretty sure she has a broken foot and an injured wing. And there's a large scrape on her side." Tony explained her injuries while he set her down on the table.

"You'll have to keep holding her for now." Asher said to Tony, but his eyes glanced toward the stairs.

"I can do that."

Asher looked at her wing first. It was tender with his touch, but the pain wasn't unbearable. Tony's hands steadied her on the table. Footsteps on the stairs pulled everyone's attention. She recognized two of the three scents that entered the room. Zachary, Ezaray, and another odd wild scent that held a similar tinge to Ezaray's. She must be Asher's mate.

"Hol..." Zachary started, but Asher cut him off.

"Officer Green brought in an injured owl. These are friends of mine, Zachary and his... Ezaray." Even Asher stumbled over the introduction. Zachary couldn't walk in here and call Holly by name in front of a human, and Asher couldn't call out someone's mate in front of him either.

"Hi there. Anthony." He introduced himself with a nod, but then turned his eyes back down to her. One finger left his hold and stroked over her head. He'd called himself Anthony rather than Tony. It suited him.

"Is she okay?" The fear flowing from Zachary hit her with such force, it filled her. It brought forth panic as she lay on a table surrounded by what felt like giants when in her small state.

"I think she will be." Then Asher reached for her foot. Holly screeched the second his fingers touched her. The pain stretched, covering her leg and more like a spider web.

"Shh. Sweet owl. I've still got you." Anthony crooned as his grip firmed, but his finger still stroked her head. His voice and the heat from his hands helped calm her. But it didn't last as Asher continued to prod at her leg.

Zachary and Ezaray crowded closer the more she squealed and whined.

"What can I do?" Zachary's frantic question barely cut through the nauseous fog swirling through her body.

"Nothing."

"Damn it, Asher." He cursed and ran his hand over his head. Ezaray came into view beside him, her hand on his arm. Zachary was her childhood friend, her hero. He'd rescued her and Ezaray. And while Holly flew off to be alone, he'd mated Ezaray. They were now more connected than she was to either of them. Of course, she was happy for them, but it didn't help the loneliness encasing her heart.

When she'd been fleeing in the woods, she'd tried to get back to Zachary, knowing she'd needed help. But now that she was here, panic overwhelmed her. It hurt too much for Asher to continue to treat her. Zachary's frustration bled into her. He tried to reach for her, shushing and soothing her as he always used to do, but Holly squirmed harder.

"She needs to stay still." Asher's calm command only worked on Anthony.

Anthony readjusted his hold and took a seat in one of the chairs surrounding the table, never losing contact with her.

"We're going to make you all better, sweet owl." Then he

hummed. His warm palms surrounded her and the vibrations coming from his throat sent a calm rhythm through her. The pain was still strong, but it was with Anthony that safety surrounded her.

Why wouldn't she feel safe with Zachary?

His scent, so strong and dizzying, her wind ruffling his hair, and the way his hands warmed her. The pieces hit her all at once. Anthony was her mate.

Fate was a fucking bitch. Holly was in no state to have a mate. She still refused to shift, preferring her freedom as an owl while she healed from her time in captivity. From what she'd learned from Zachary, it was pointless to fight it. And that just made her angrier at Fate and her meddling. She could have sent any other conservation officer to get her, then she'd be in Zachary's hands and perfectly comfortable. But no. Panic at the thought of anyone other than her mate touching her pulsed hard.

"Okay," Asher spoke to her, "I'm going to give you something for the pain so I can reset your leg and bandage you up. It will probably put you to sleep, too."

She pushed herself further into Anthony's hands. There was nothing she could do but accept their help. As long as her mate didn't leave, she knew she'd be okay.

Asher inserted the needle and the owl screeched, her muscles tensing for a moment before she relaxed against Anthony's palms. She'd have a reprieve from her pain. Only moments later her swirling eyes drifted closed, and she fell asleep. Anthony loosened his grip but kept one hand near her head to continue to stroke her feathers. The others that had entered the room were beside themselves, clearly having a strong connection to the animal on the table. He found their behaviour odd, but Anthony let it go. His concern was for his owl.

His owl.

She'd calmed in his arms, in his hands. He felt he had a responsibility toward her. She'd pushed toward him when the others tried to reach for her. Anthony had intended to take her to the rescue once Asher had treated her, knowing that would be the best place for her to recover, but he could no longer do that. Besides, he suspected the other men in the room would argue with his plan.

Was he really going to take her home and care for her himself?

Zachary paced the room while Asher worked, and Ezaray sat at the opposite side of the table. Gwen, Asher's wife, cooked dinner behind them all. The room felt filled with noise, a hum of anxiety, but no one spoke until Asher finished.

"I set her leg. It will heal fine. She has a sprained wing and the scrape in her side isn't deep. It will be sore, though." Asher stretched his back, then started cleaning up.

"Thanks for looking after her, especially in your own home."

"It's not the first time."

"What do I need to take care of her?" All eyes in the kitchen turned on Anthony. He'd figured he'd get some resistance based on the reactions of all the extra people that worried for the owl.

"She can stay here. We'll look after her." Zachary took a few steps toward him, his eyes darkening and ready for a fight. Anthony twisted his lips while mulling over his options. It would be easier to leave her here. She'd be in better care with a veterinarian. He wouldn't get in a fight with an angry guy. But that sense of responsibility for her jumped to the surface. He wanted to take care of her.

"That's a nice offer, thank you. But it's no burden. I found her and am responsible for her." He hadn't meant to admit that.

"I'm responsible for her." The words sounded like they hurt.

"How so?"

Zachary clamped his jaw shut and looked to Asher, who only raised his brow. They knew what each of them wanted to say, but they left Anthony in the dark.

"Have either of you seen this owl before?" Alarm bells installed by his career piqued his curiosity.

"Yes," they answered in unison.

"No rehabilitation centre, please, as we know her home is here. She'll heal well." Asher stepped in front of Zachary. The silence stretched before Anthony answered. Zachary struggled behind Asher who remained calm with steady eyes on Anthony. Gwen and Ezaray both held their breath while looking between Anthony and the other men.

"No centre," Anthony agreed. Asher and Zachary both had strong opinions about this specific owl, but he didn't much care for the idea of parting with her. "What do I need to take care of her?" Anthony pulled out his officer voice to warn them both he was serious about taking her. She'd put her trust in him. He couldn't abandon her.

Zachary tensed, but Asher sighed and gave him instructions. "A large space, no small cage. You can feed her chicken or fish until she's able to hunt on her own. But at that point she'll be on her own, anyway."

"Thank you. I'd appreciate it if you came to check up on her."

"Of course. I'll swing by in the morning."

Anthony cradled the owl as he lifted her.

"I'll come with you and hold her while you drive." Zachary offered, his tone subdued.

"Thank you." Anthony took the peace offering. "I don't live that far. I can drive you back once I have her settled."

"No need."

Anthony said his goodbyes to Asher, Gwen, and Ezaray. Zachary followed him out to his truck. He passed the owl over to him, surprised at his own reluctance to let her go, but pleased she was still unconscious. Her reaction to Zachary inside worried him.

"How long have you known Asher?" Anthony backed out of the driveway and turned the truck around.

"Not long." Zachary looked down at the owl with concern. His eyes never left her.

"You're not from Alder Ridge, are you?" There weren't many people Anthony didn't know, but Alder Ridge wasn't so big you couldn't tell who didn't belong.

"I'm from Hull Creek."

"What brought you down our way?"

"That's a long story." One he didn't want to tell. Anthony let the conversation drop. Zachary didn't want to talk, and Anthony couldn't figure out why he was trying so hard.

Reaching the end of the long lane that led to Asher's, Anthony slowed to look for traffic on the main road before cutting across to the next lane that led to his place. He wasn't so far into the woods as Asher, but he had the same privacy. Something he needed. The time to be alone, away from the town, from prying family and neighbors. Oh, he enjoyed living where he grew up, but he'd been here long enough and chose a profession that kept him under scrutiny. Coming home was his heaven, his peace.

He parked his truck under his tree. When he reached the other side of the truck, Zachary had his door open and was stepping out. "You go unlock. I can carry her in."

Anthony opened his door and allowed Zachary to follow him in. He stopped in his living room and spun around, trying to think of the best setup. Mentally snapping his fingers, he grabbed the spare playpen his sister left during her last visit. He set it up against the wall by his back door that led to the deck and lined the bottom with a couple blankets.

"There. What do you think?" He slapped his fists on his hips and looked at Zachary.

"She'll hate it. She'd be fine with just the blankets on the floor."

"True, but I don't want her doing anything that will cause her more harm."

"I suppose so." His reluctance to agree was evident in the pinch of his lips and the tightening of his jaw.

Anthony took the owl from Zachary and placed her in the centre of the playpen. "I can give you a ride back to Asher's."

"That's okay. It's not that far. I'll walk."

"If you're sure."

"Yeah." He hesitated. "If you need any help with her, you can call me, too." He lifted a pen and paper off the end table and wrote on it before setting it back down. "That's my number."

"I will. Thanks for the help getting her here."

Zachary nodded, and after one last glance at the owl, he left.

"Well, I guess it's just you and me." Anthony stroked her head to see if she would stir, but not a single movement other than her tiny breathing. He eyed his couch, happy he went with comfort rather than aesthetics because that would be his bed for the next few nights.

WOUNDED WINDS SERIES

White Bonds
Auburn Ties
Silver Chains
Amber Oath
Emerald Promise
Golden Vow

ABOUT THE AUTHOR

Looking at a crossroads, Sarah chose to write. With a deep love of anything romance, it was natural that romance stories flowed into her journal. From the East Coast and living in Alberta, Canada, she enjoys life with her family and the beauty of the province around her. She gets hilariously excited when new stories and characters pop in her head and can't wait to write them out whether in the sub-genres of romantic suspense or paranormal romance. She hopes her readers enjoy her stories as much as she enjoys writing them.

You can find Sarah on Facebook and Instagram @authorsarahu, in her reader group *Sarah's Wild Ones,* and on BookBub.